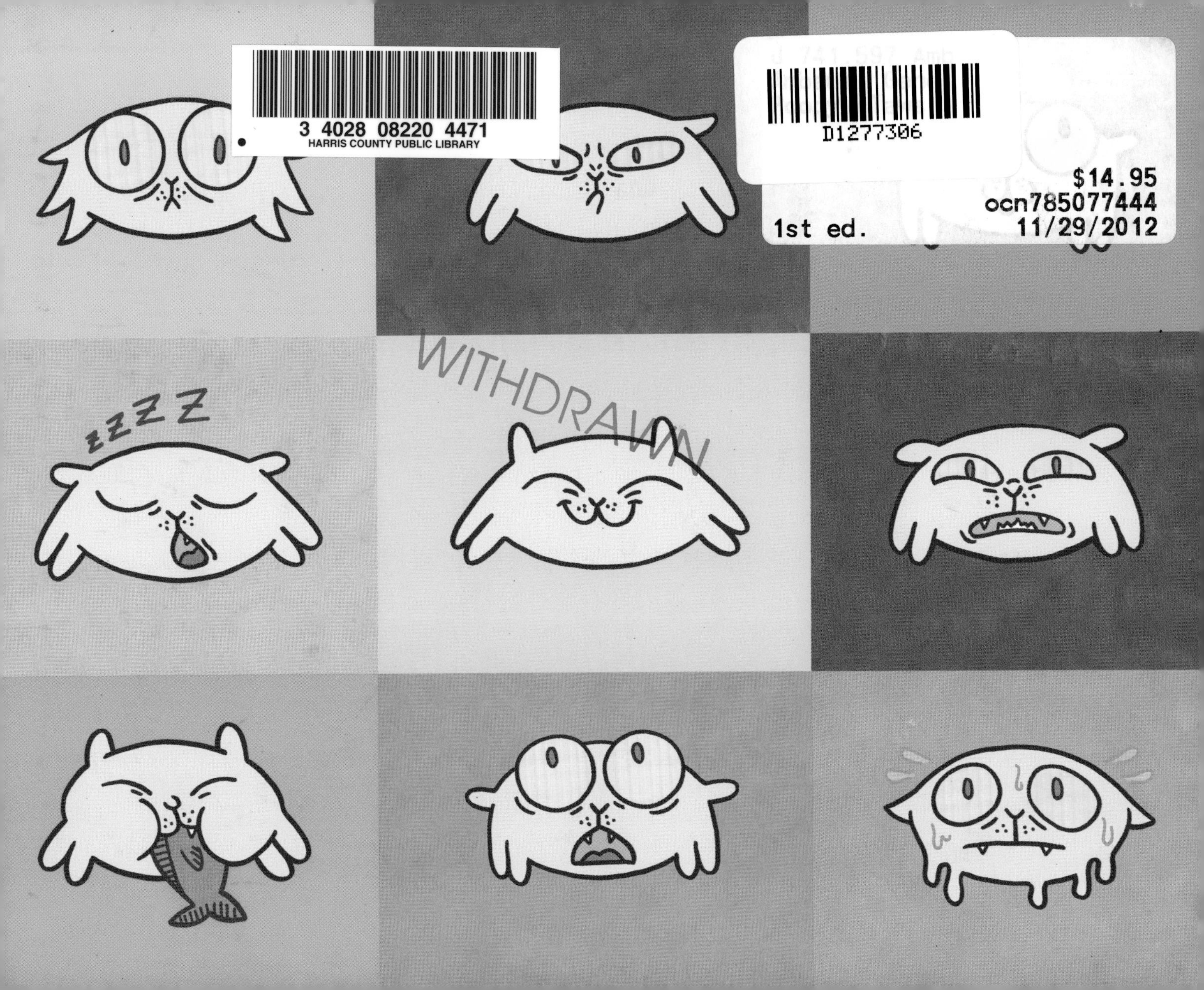
ZZZZ

POOPY CLAWS

written by Gene Ambaum

illustrated by Sophie Goldstein

Overdue Media, LLC Seattle, Washington

For my grandmother, who has a sick sense of humor and an overflowing litter box.
-Gene

For furry companions future and past. For Sammy.
-Sophie

Overdue Media, LLC 4819 S Oregon Street Seattle, WA 98118
www.overduemedia.com geneambaum@gmail.com

Printed in China

Publisher's Cataloging-in-Publication data
Goldstein, Sophie, and Ambaum, Gene.
Poopy Claws / Sophie Goldstein and Gene Ambaum.
52 p. : col. ill ; 18 cm
ISBN 978-0-9740353-9-0
1. Cats -- Comic books, strips, etc.
2. Feces -- Juvenile literature.

First Edition, First Printing 1 2 3 4 5 6 7 8 9 10

This is a work of fiction. If it reminds you of any people or any cats
you've known, that's pure coincidence.

And, well, yuck.

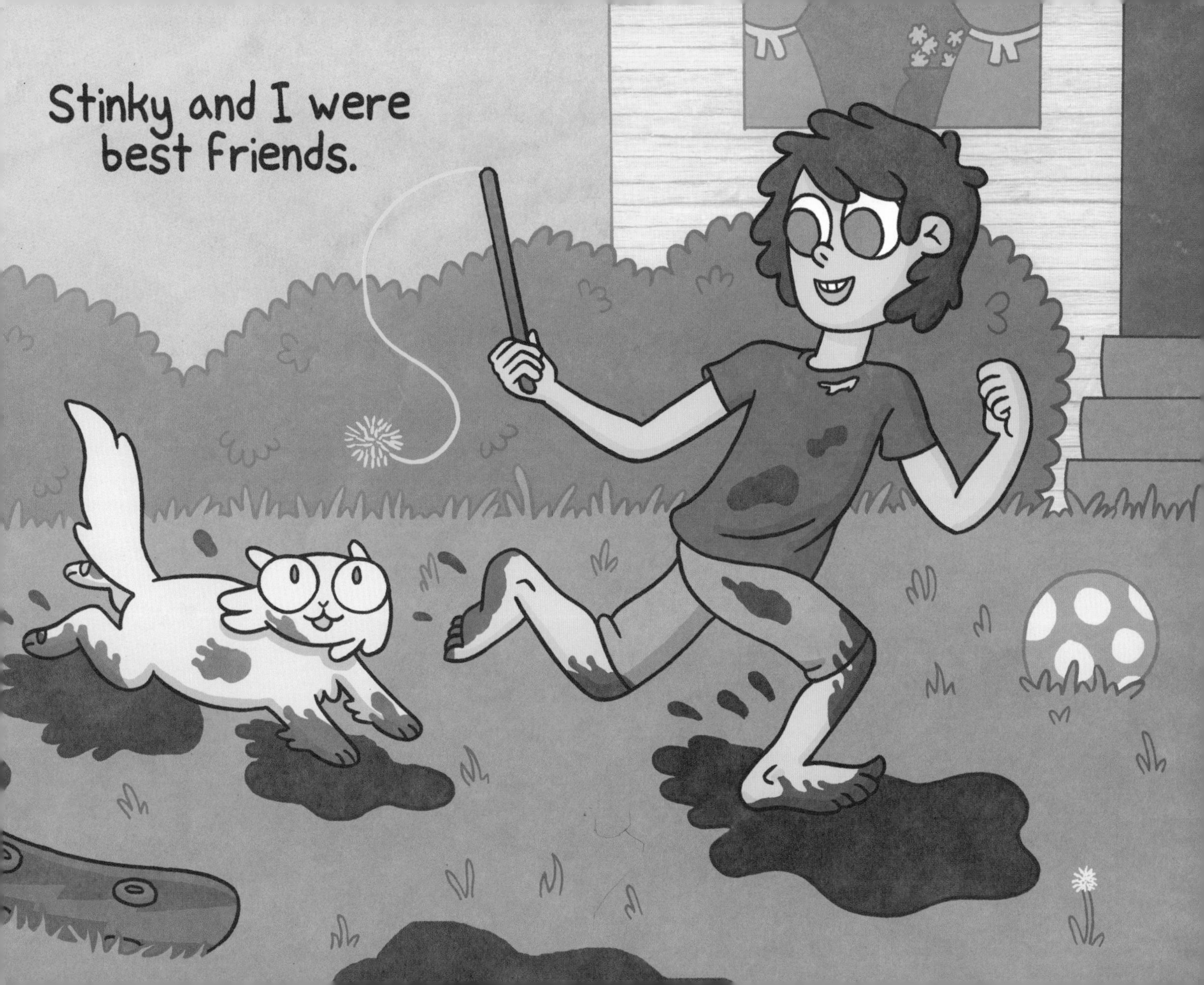
Stinky and I were best friends.

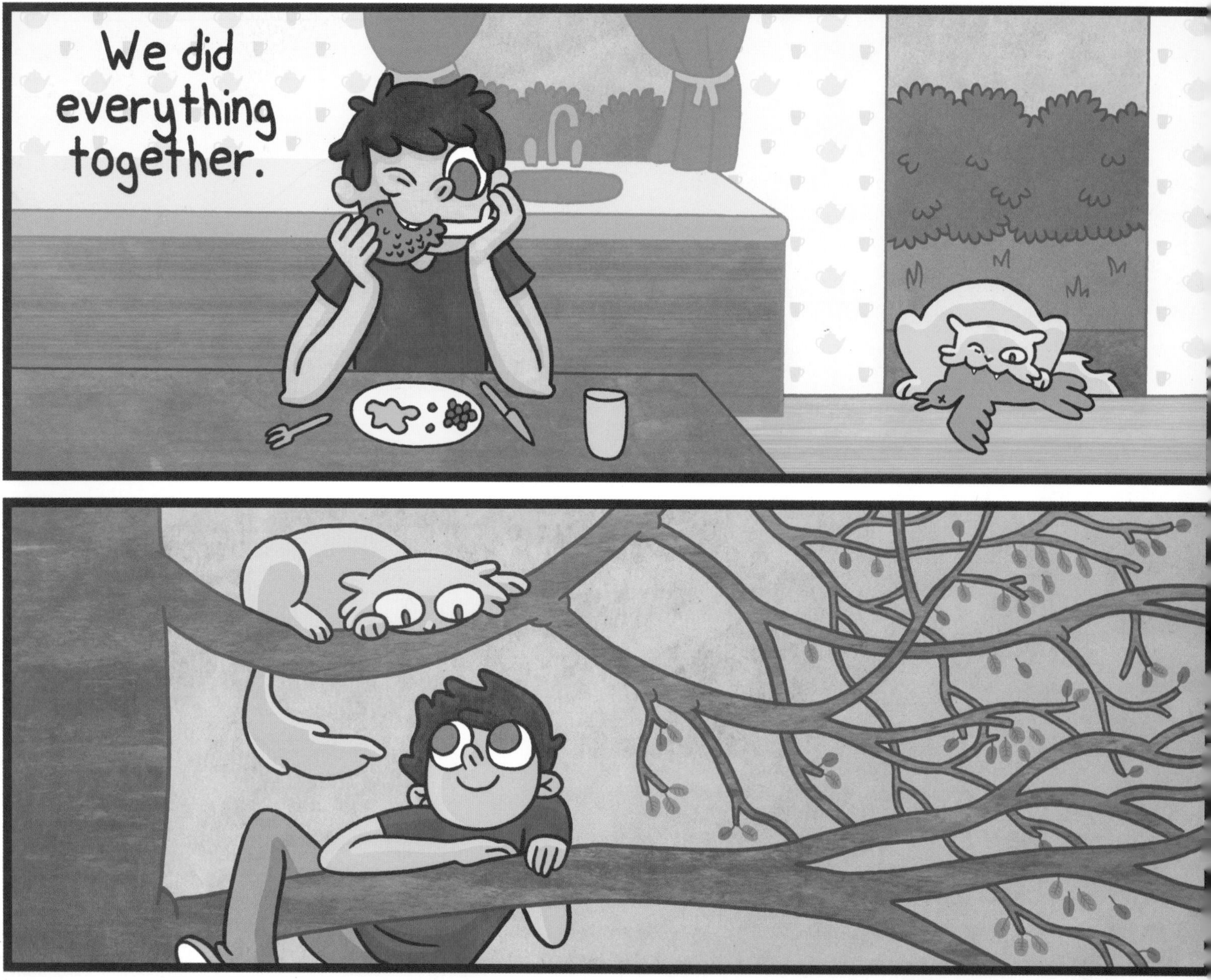
We did everything together.

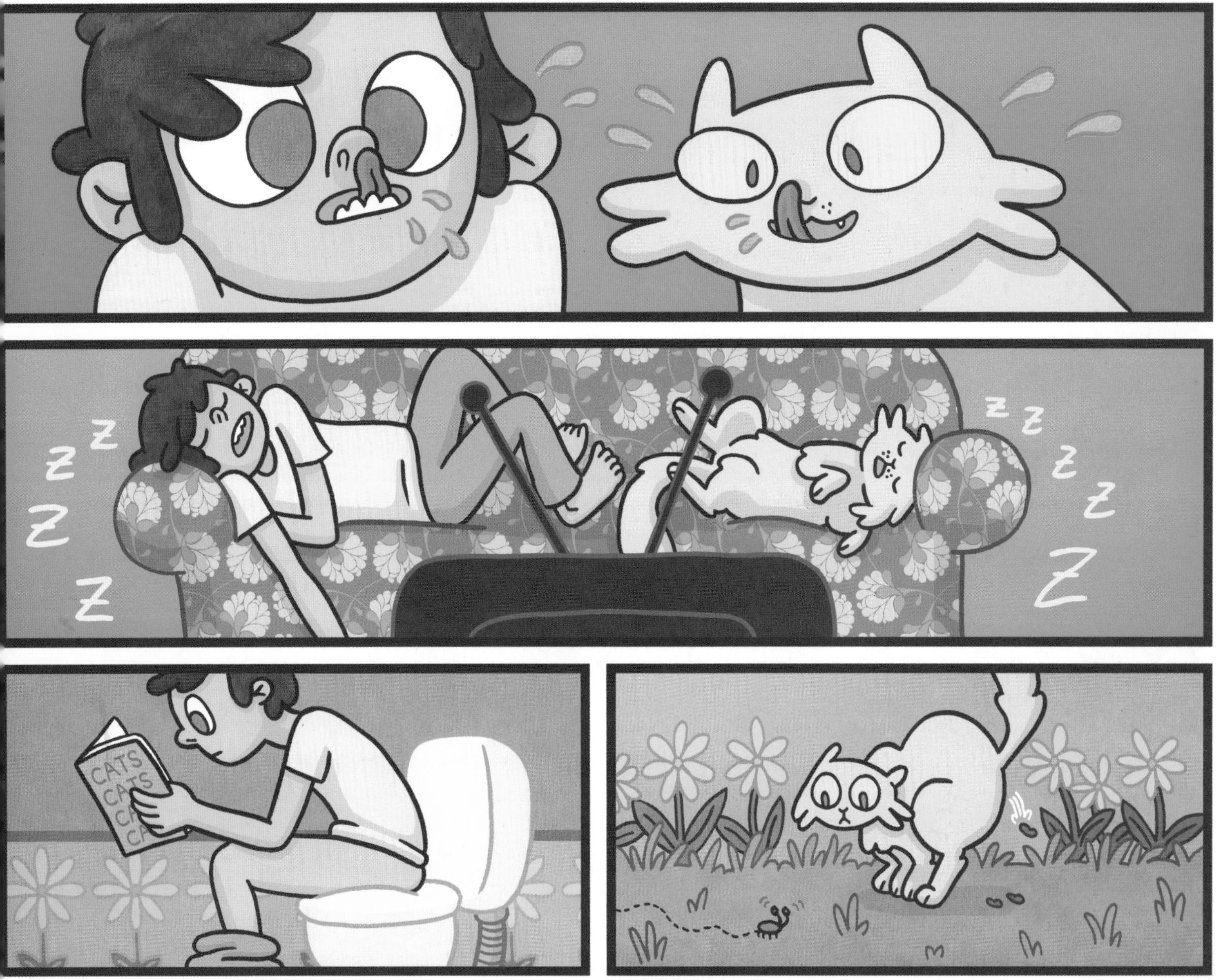
Z Z Z Z
Z Z Z Z Z
CATS
CATS
CA
CA

Mom didn't like us getting dirty.

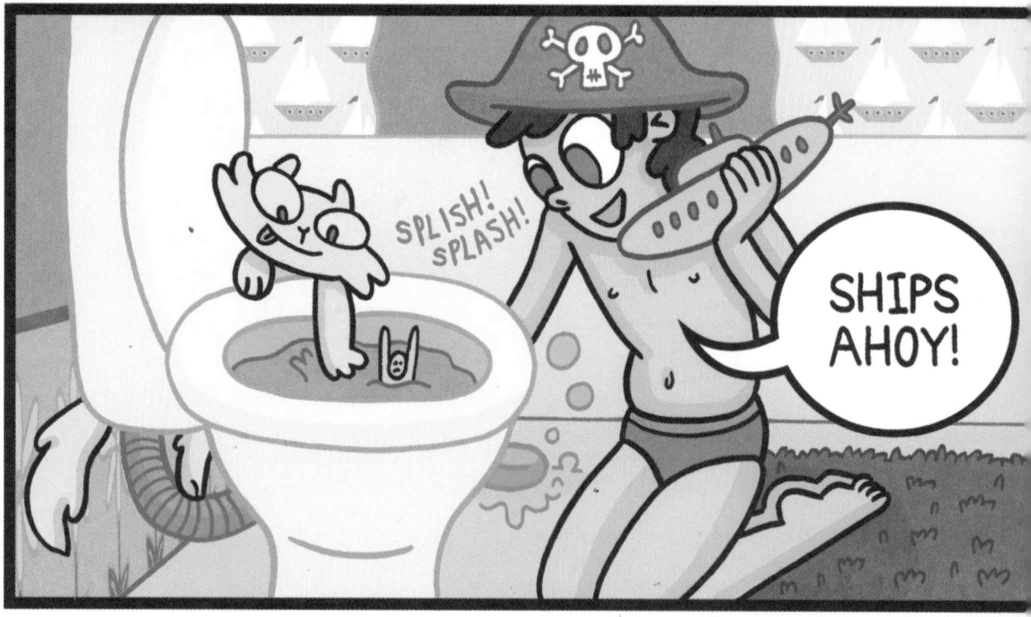
SPLISH! SPLASH!
SHIPS AHOY!

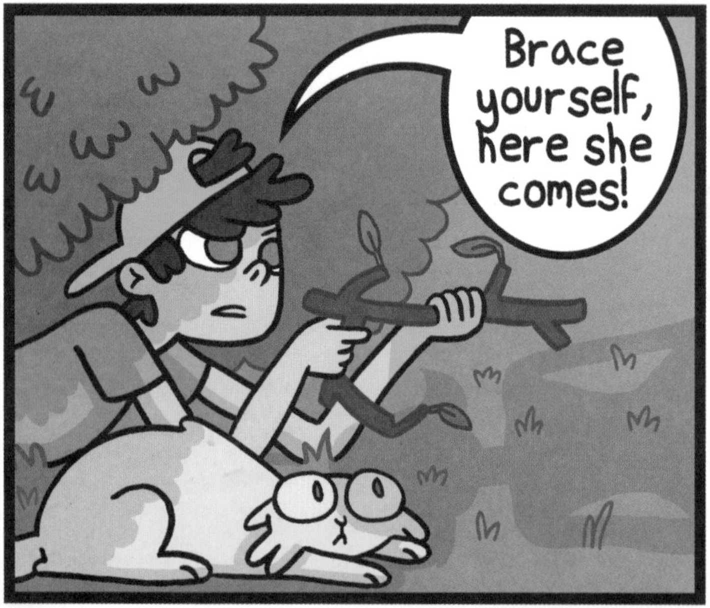
Brace yourself, here she comes!

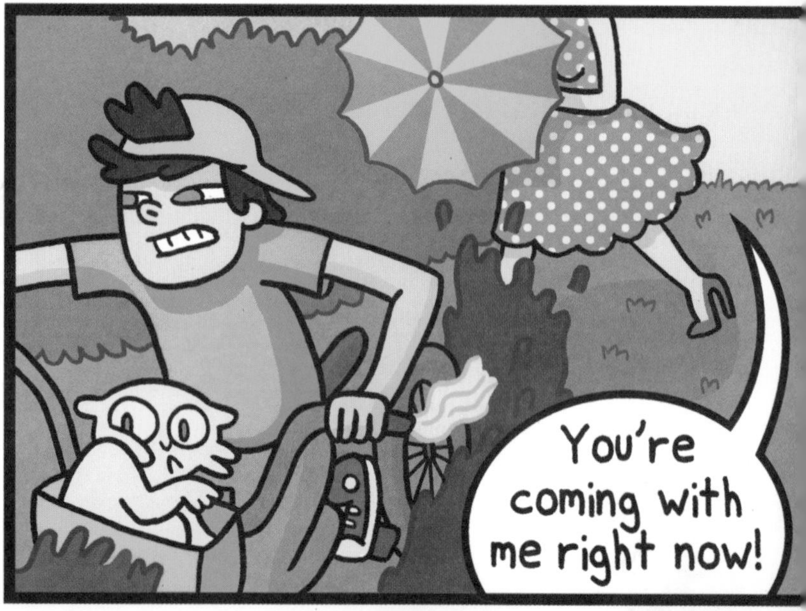
You're coming with me right now!

But nothing made her as mad as Stinky not using his litter box.

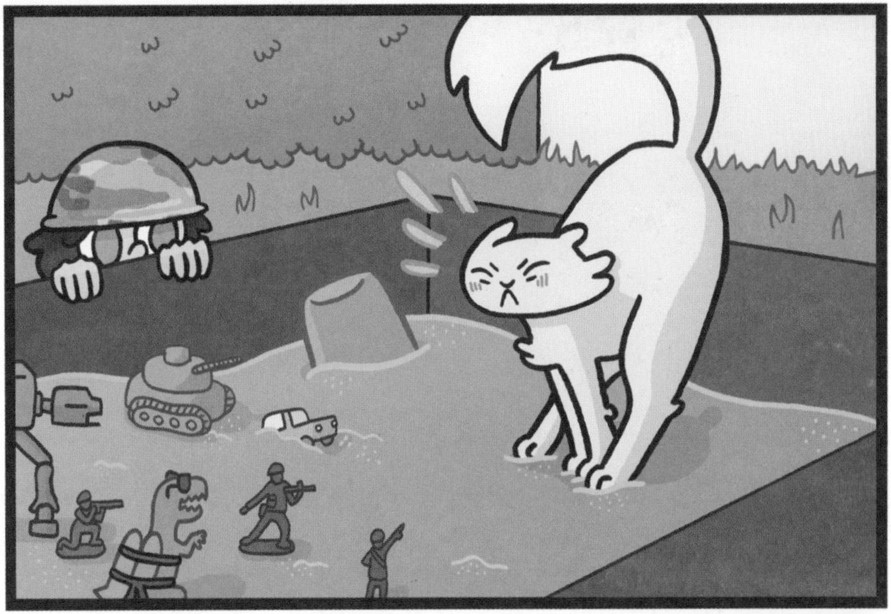

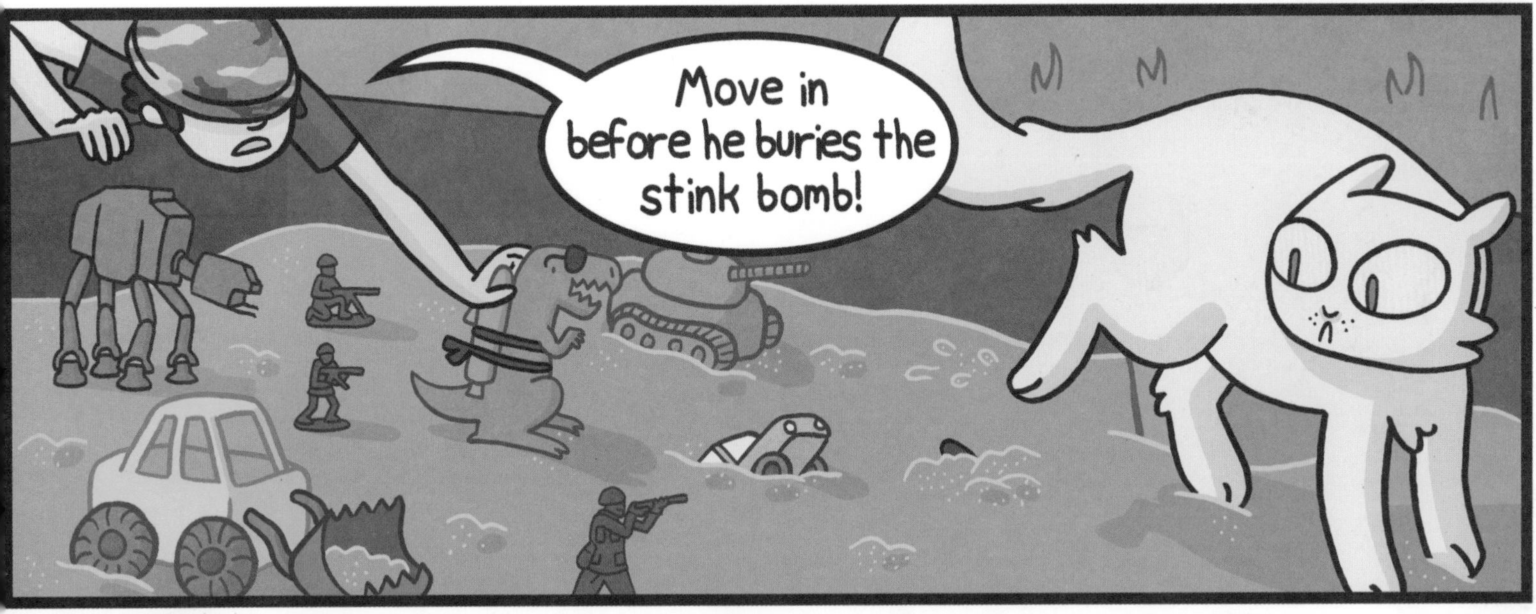
Move in before he buries the stink bomb!

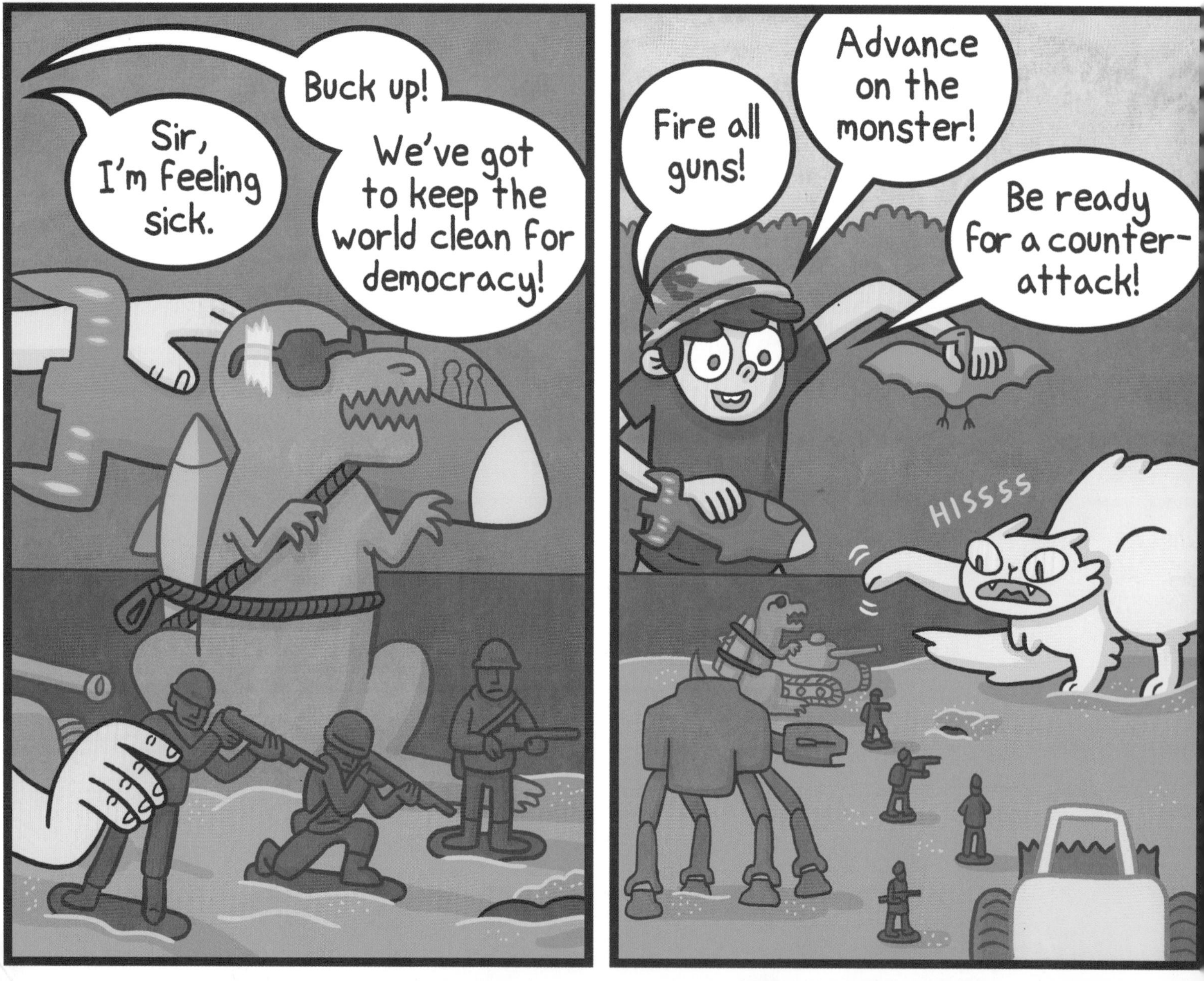
Sir, I'm feeling sick.
Buck up!
We've got to keep the world clean for democracy!
Fire all guns!
Advance on the monster!
Be ready for a counter-attack!
HISSSS

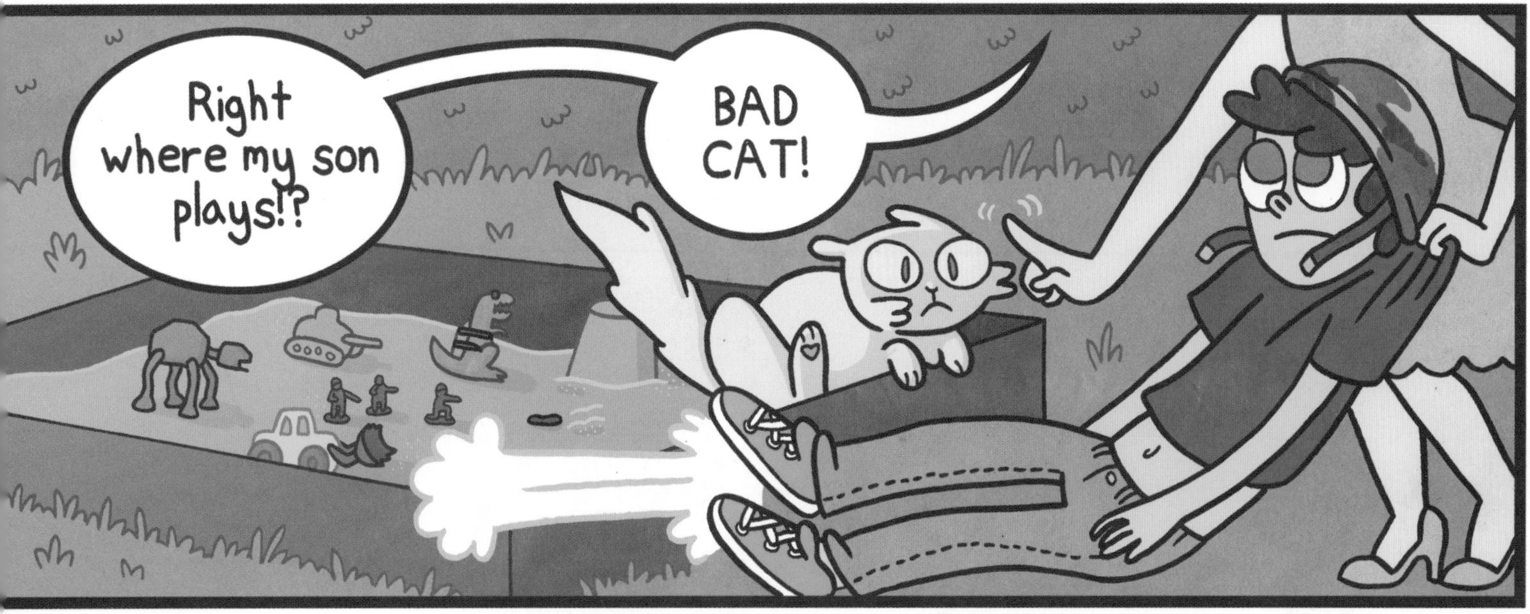
Right where my son plays!?
BAD CAT!

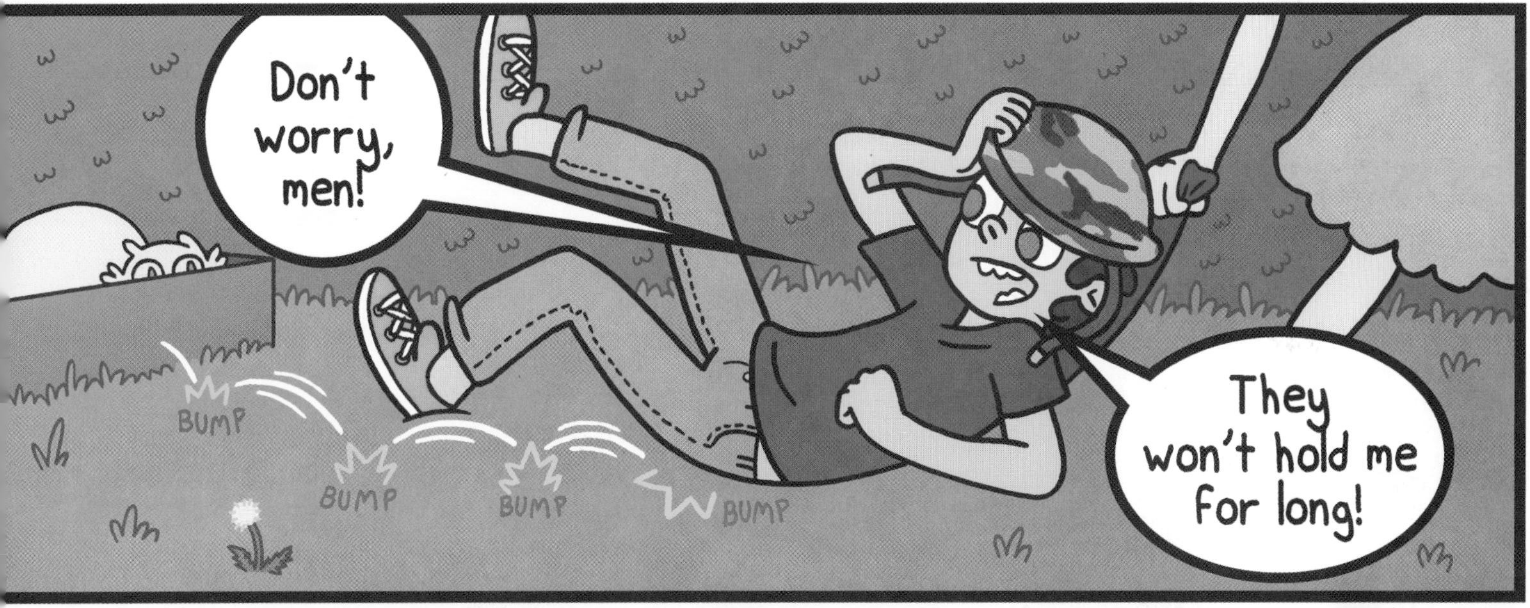
Don't worry, men!
BUMP
BUMP
BUMP
BUMP
They won't hold me for long!

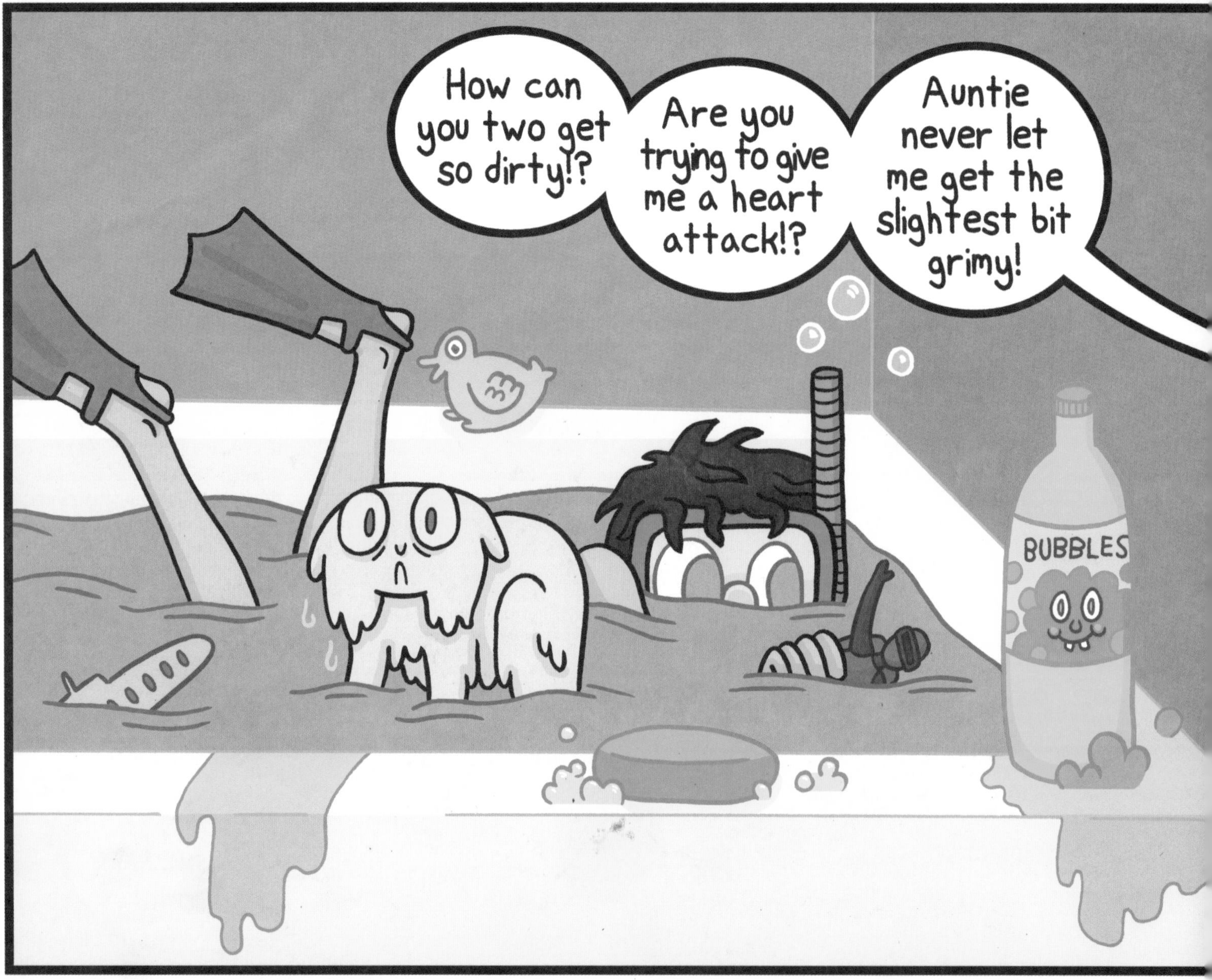
How can you two get so dirty!?
Are you trying to give me a heart attack!?
Auntie never let me get the slightest bit grimy!
BUBBLES

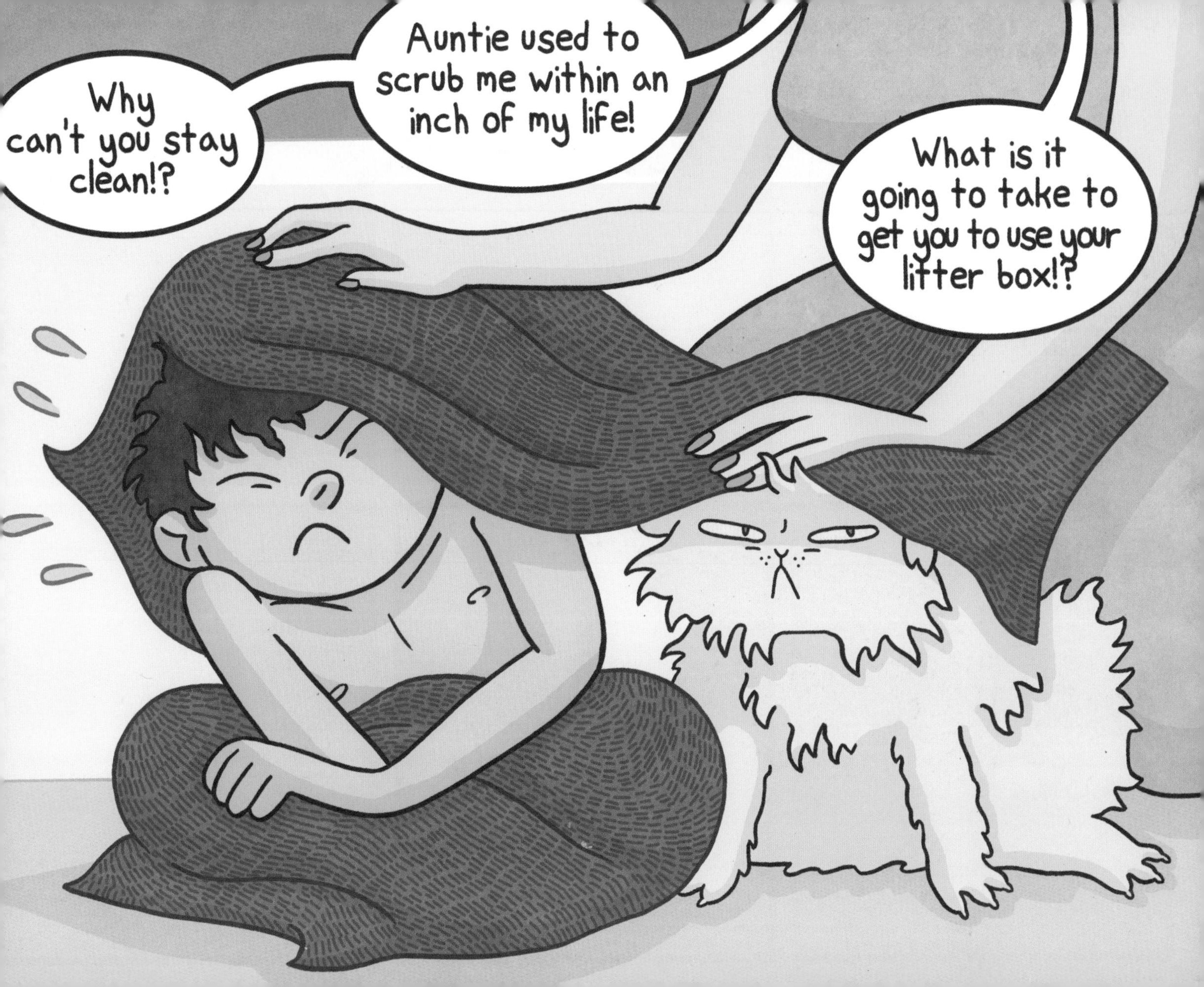
Why can't you stay clean!?
Auntie used to scrub me within an inch of my life!
What is it going to take to get you to use your litter box!?

Dad tried everything to make the litter box more appealing.

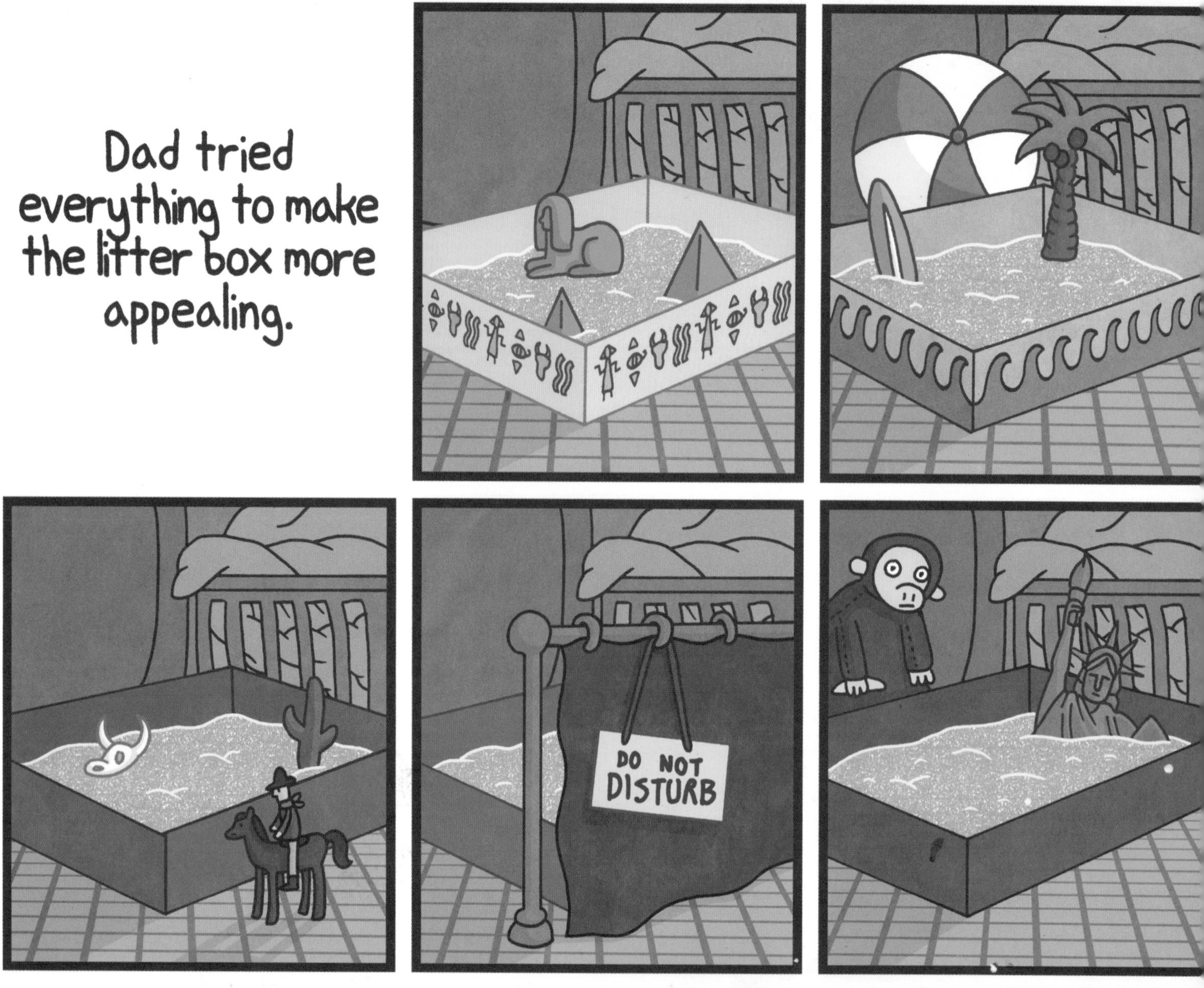
DO NOT DISTURB

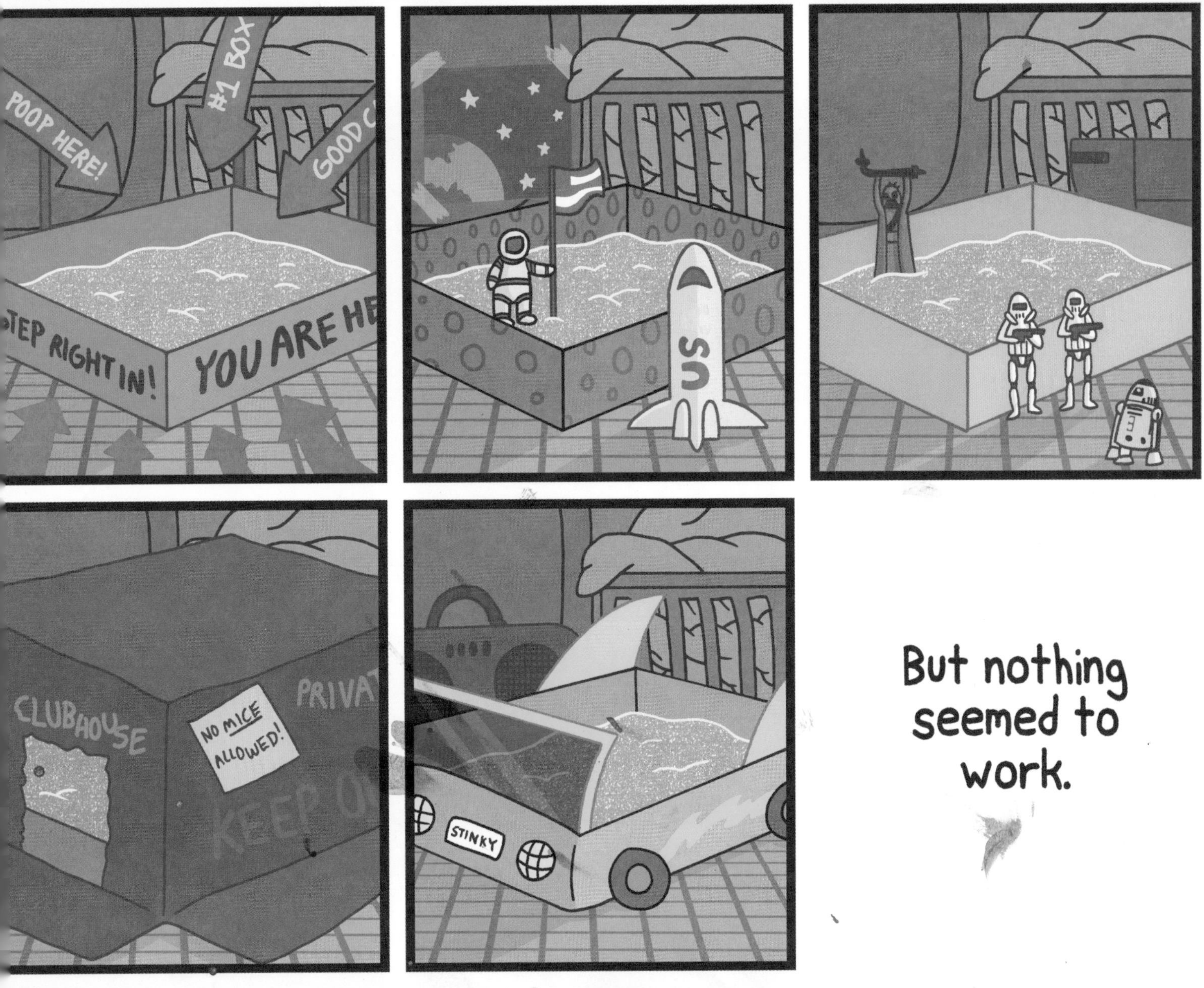
POOP HERE!
#1 BOX
US
CLUBHOUSE
NO MICE ALLOWED!
STINKY
But nothing seemed to work.

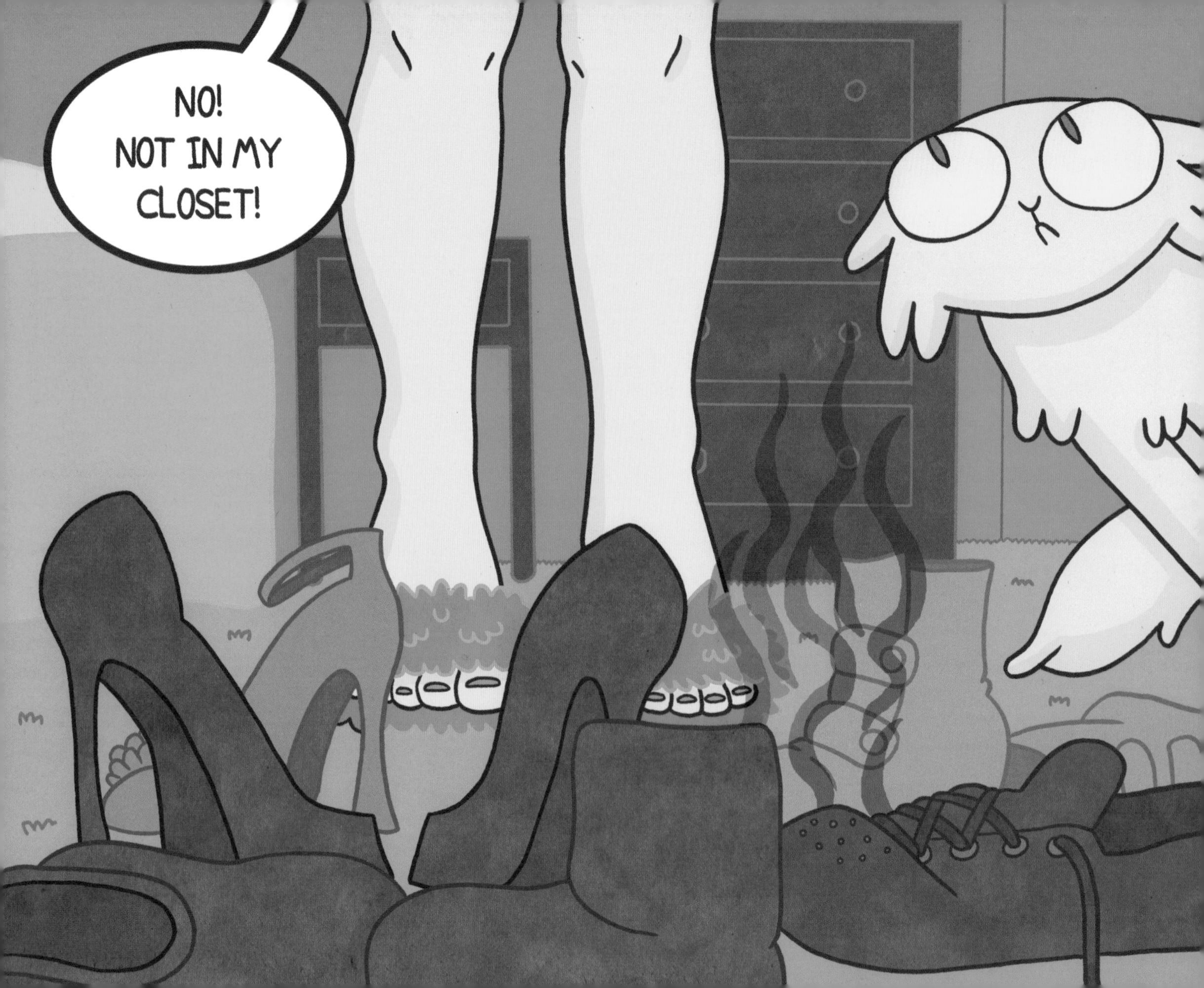
NO! NOT IN MY CLOSET!

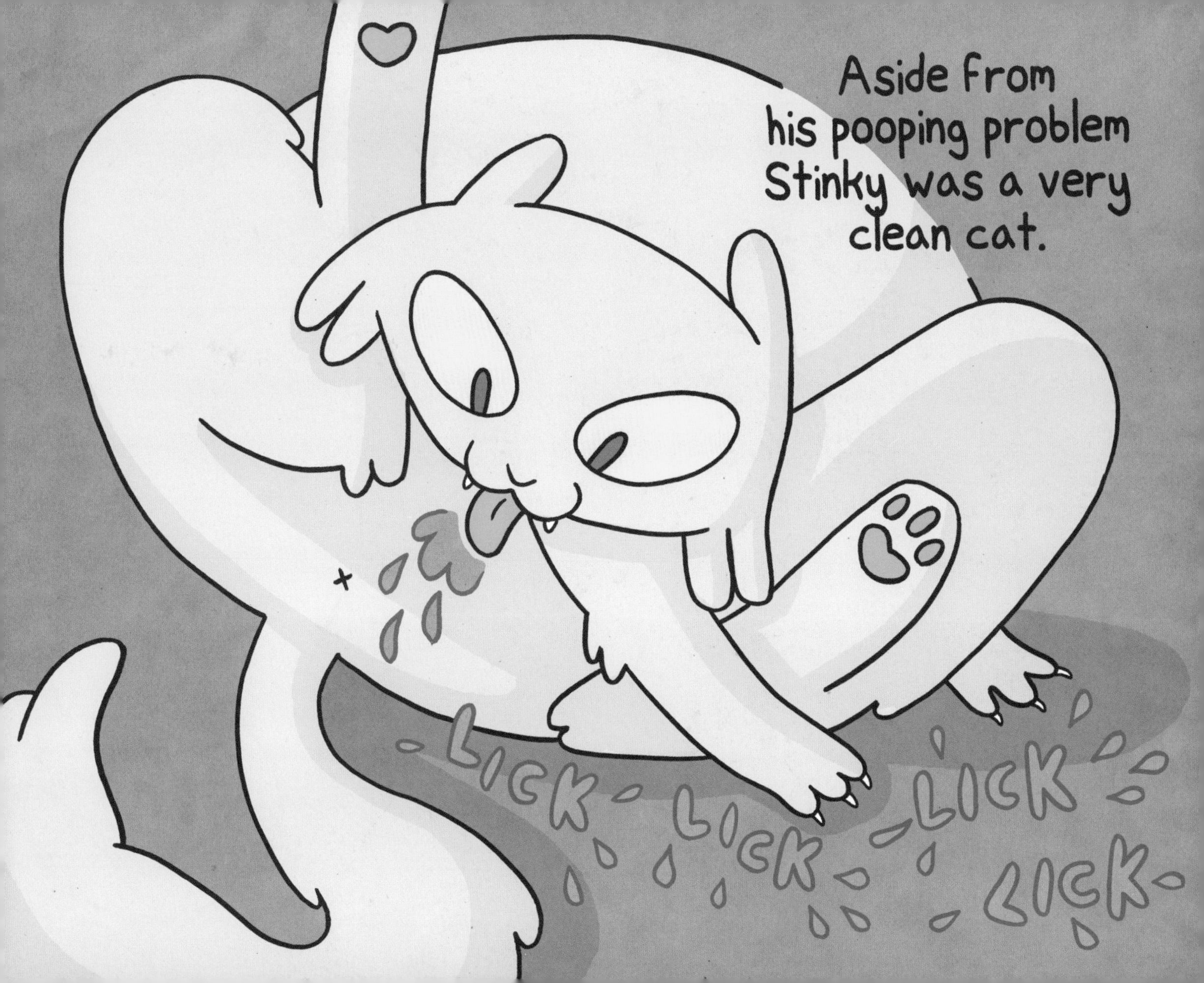
Aside from his pooping problem Stinky was a very clean cat.
LICK
LICK
LICK
LICK

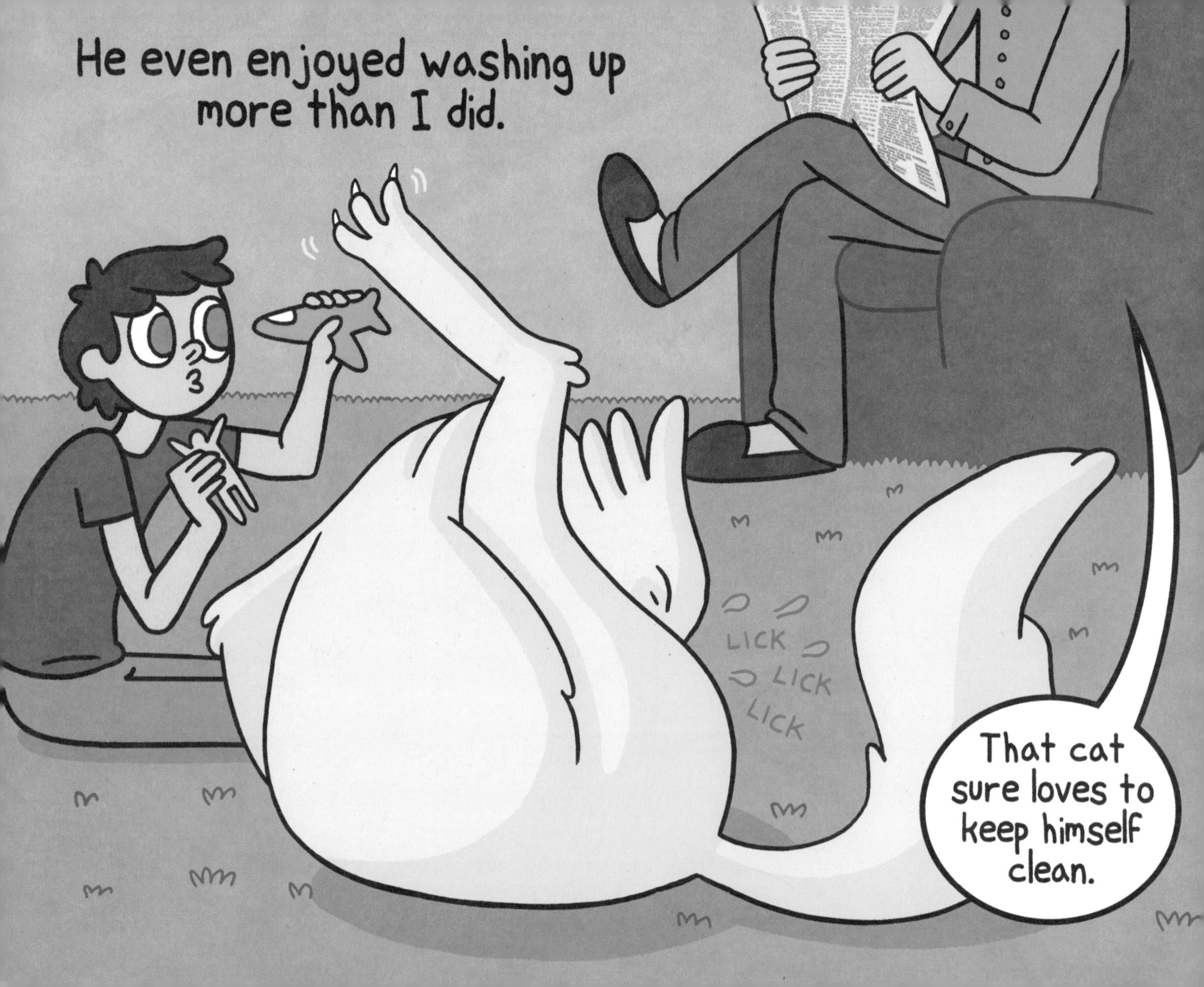
He even enjoyed washing up more than I did.
LICK LICK LICK
That cat sure loves to keep himself clean.

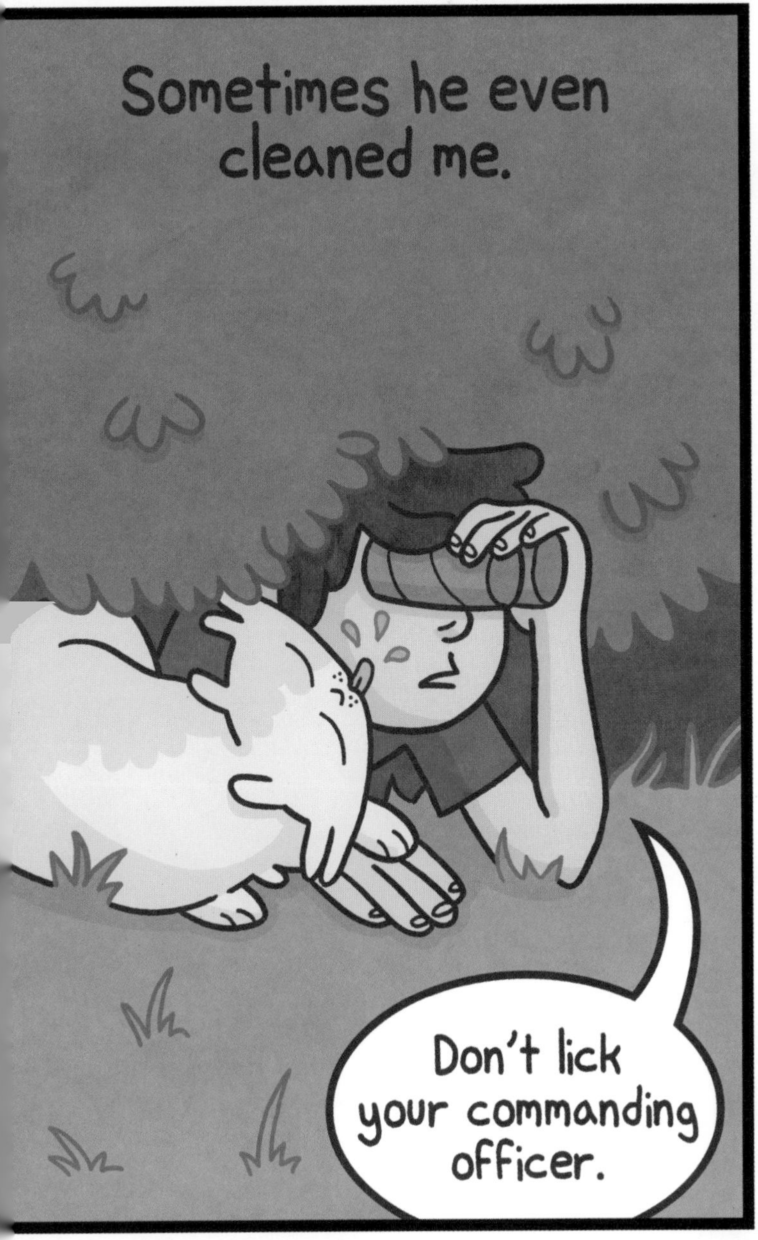
Sometimes he even cleaned me.
Don't lick your commanding officer.

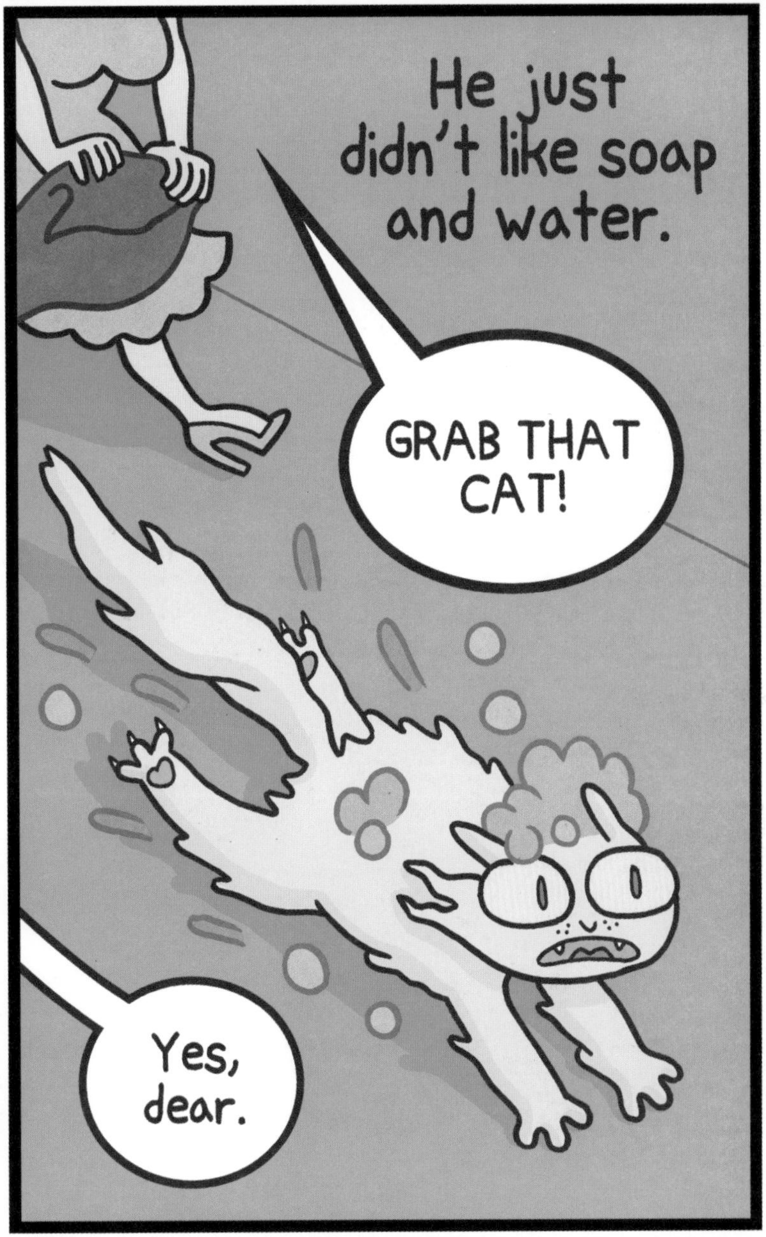
He just didn't like soap and water.
GRAB THAT CAT!
Yes, dear.

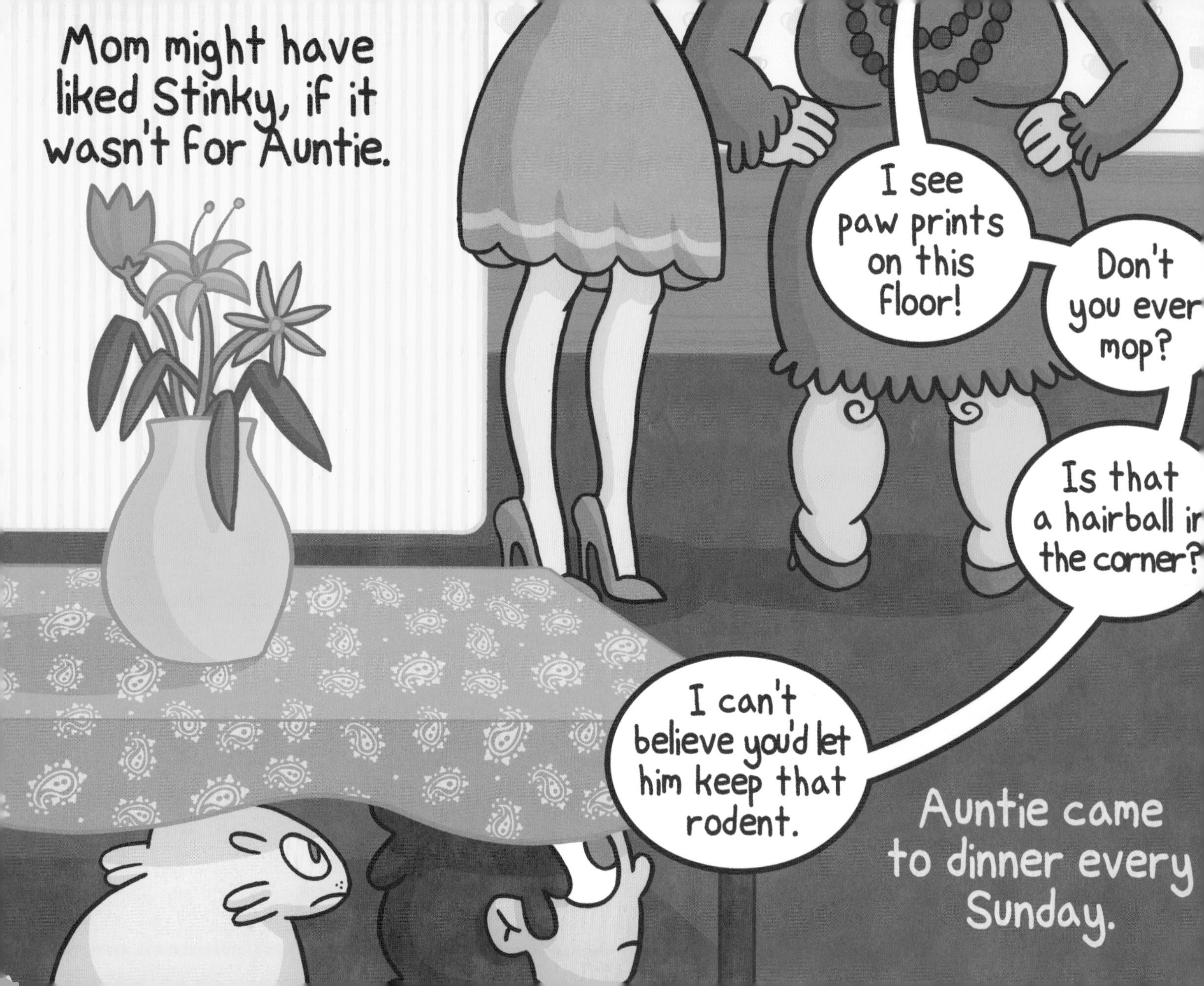

Mom might have liked Stinky, if it wasn't for Auntie.
I see paw prints on this floor!
Don't you ever mop?
Is that a hairball in the corner?
I can't believe you'd let him keep that rodent.
Auntie came to dinner every Sunday.

And unfortunately, today was Sunday.

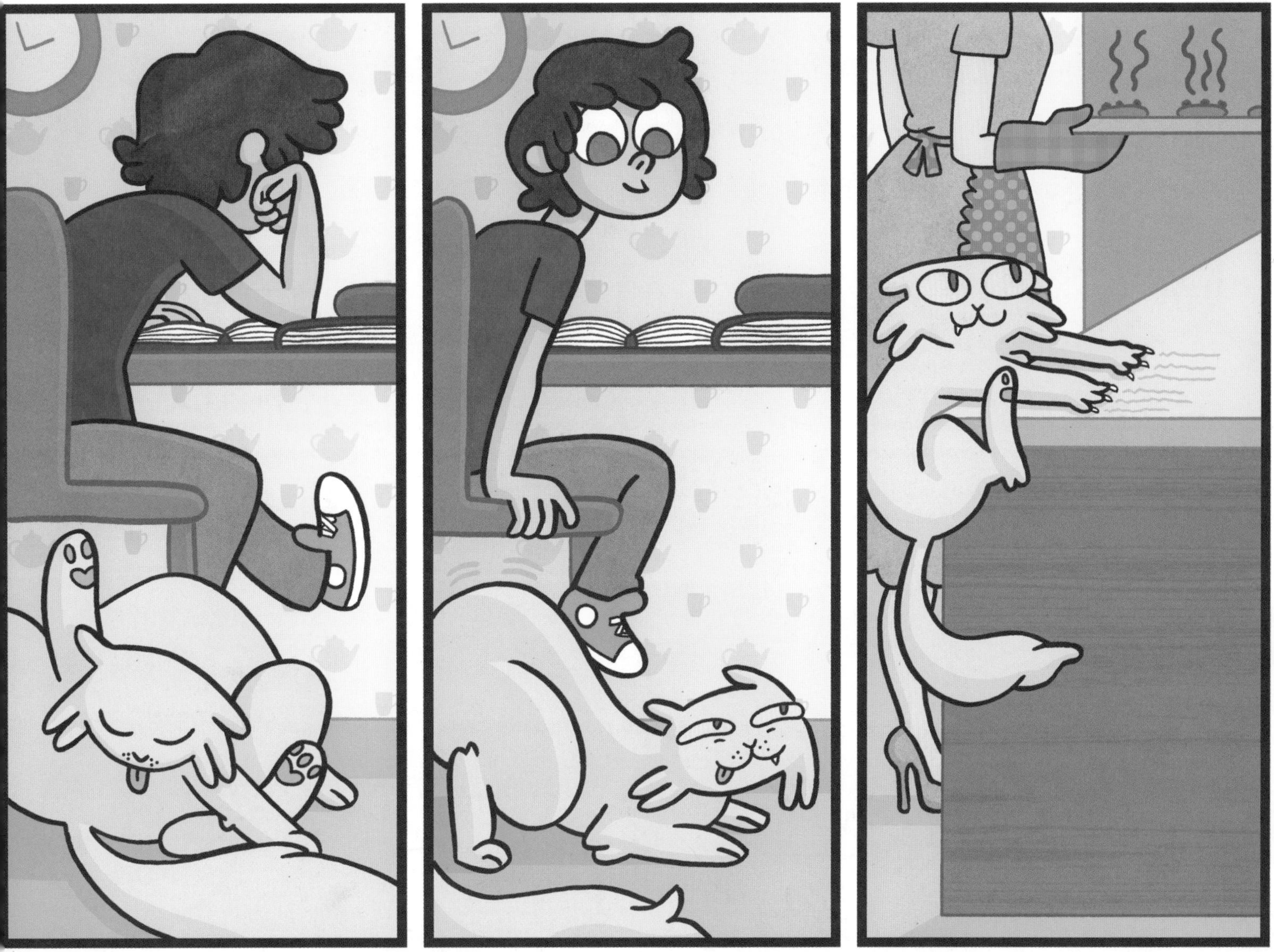

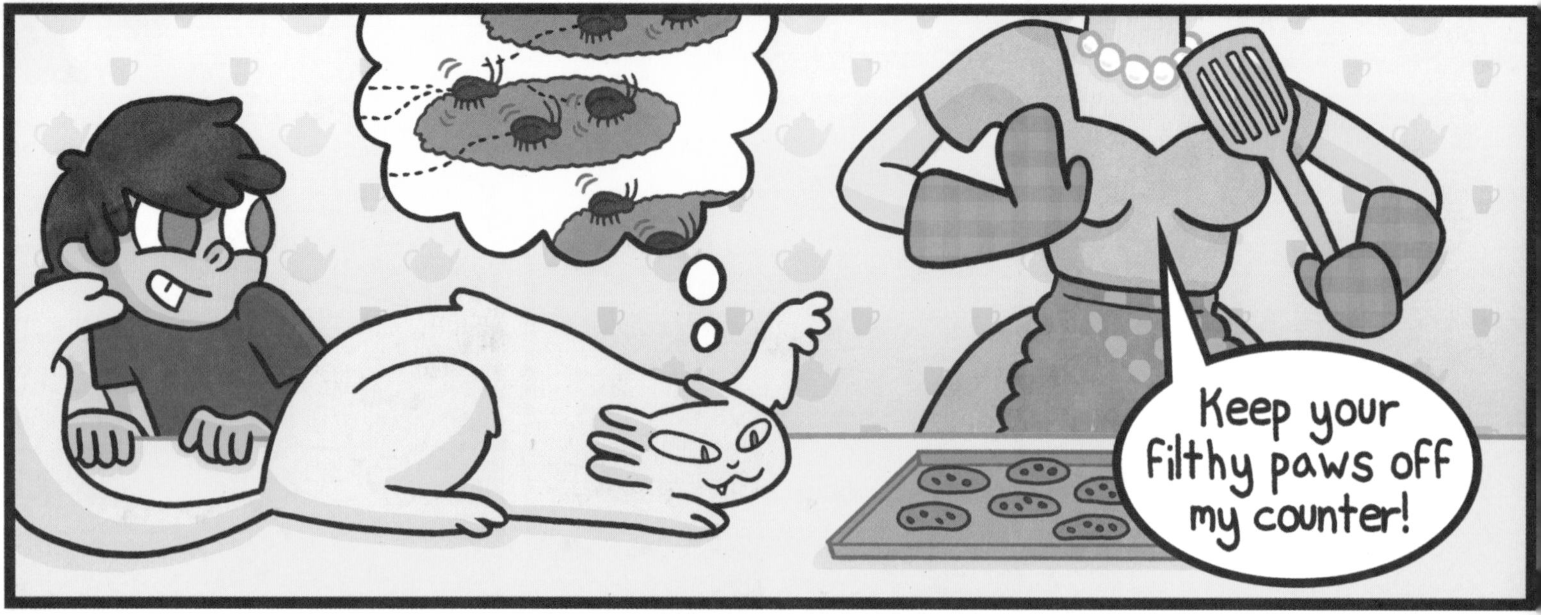
Keep your filthy paws off my counter!

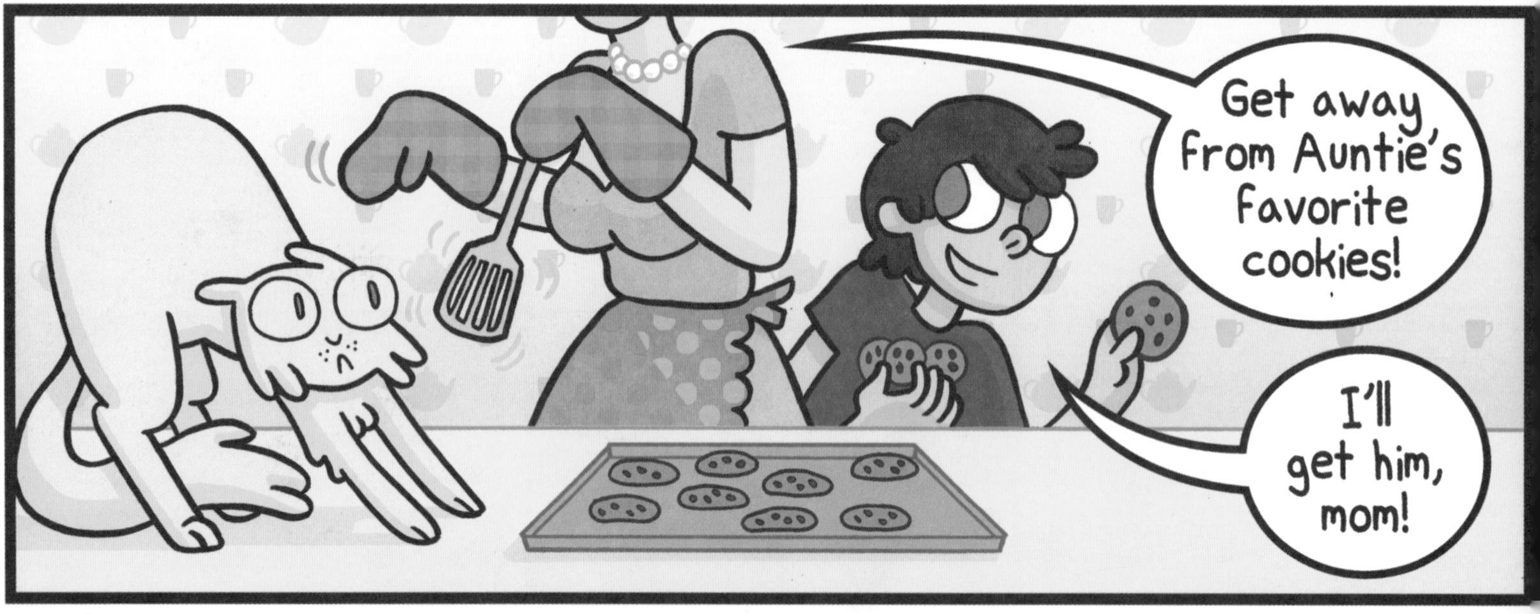
Get away from Auntie's favorite cookies!
I'll get him, mom!

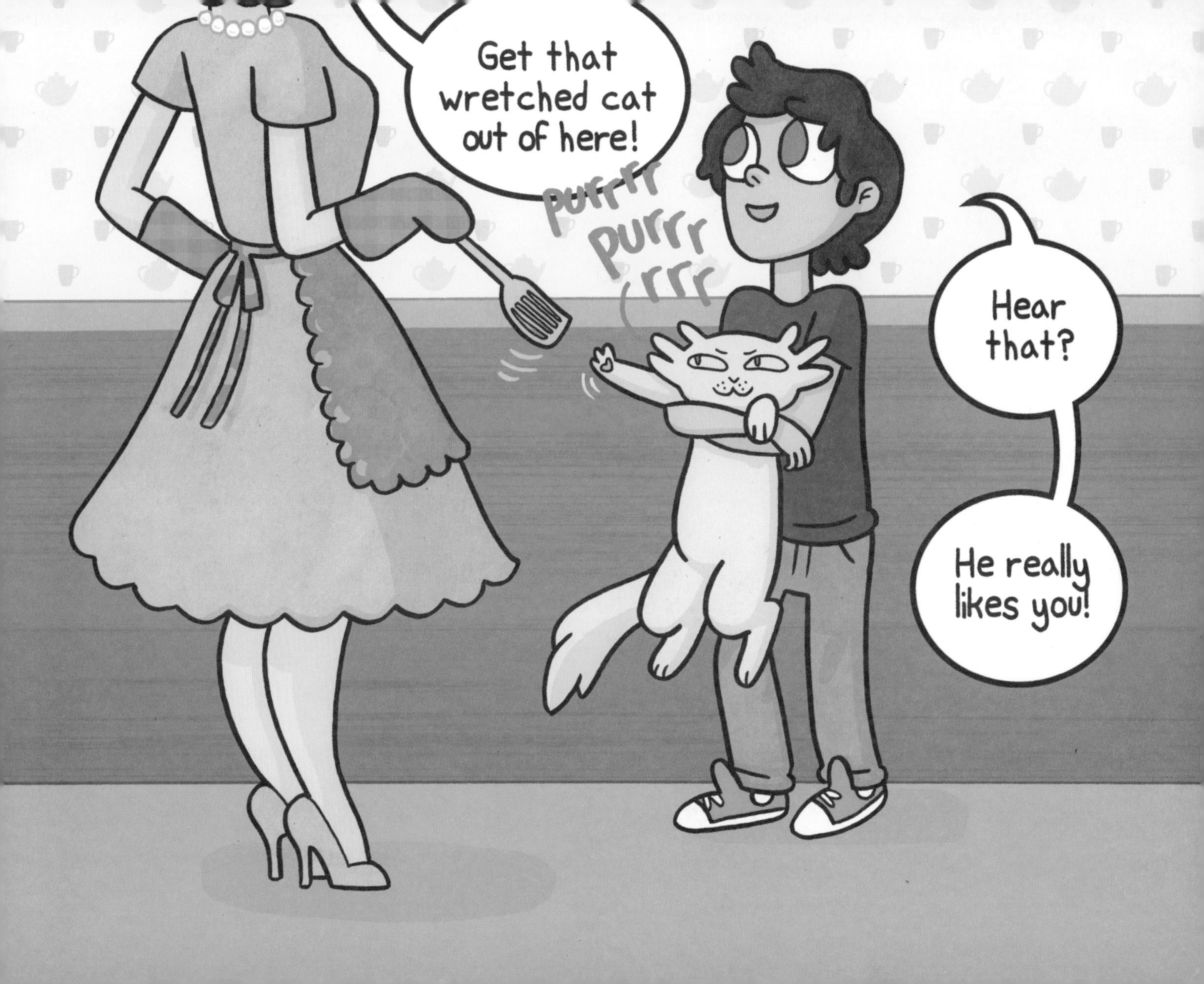
Get that wretched cat out of here!
purrrr
purrrr
rrrr
Hear that?
He really likes you!

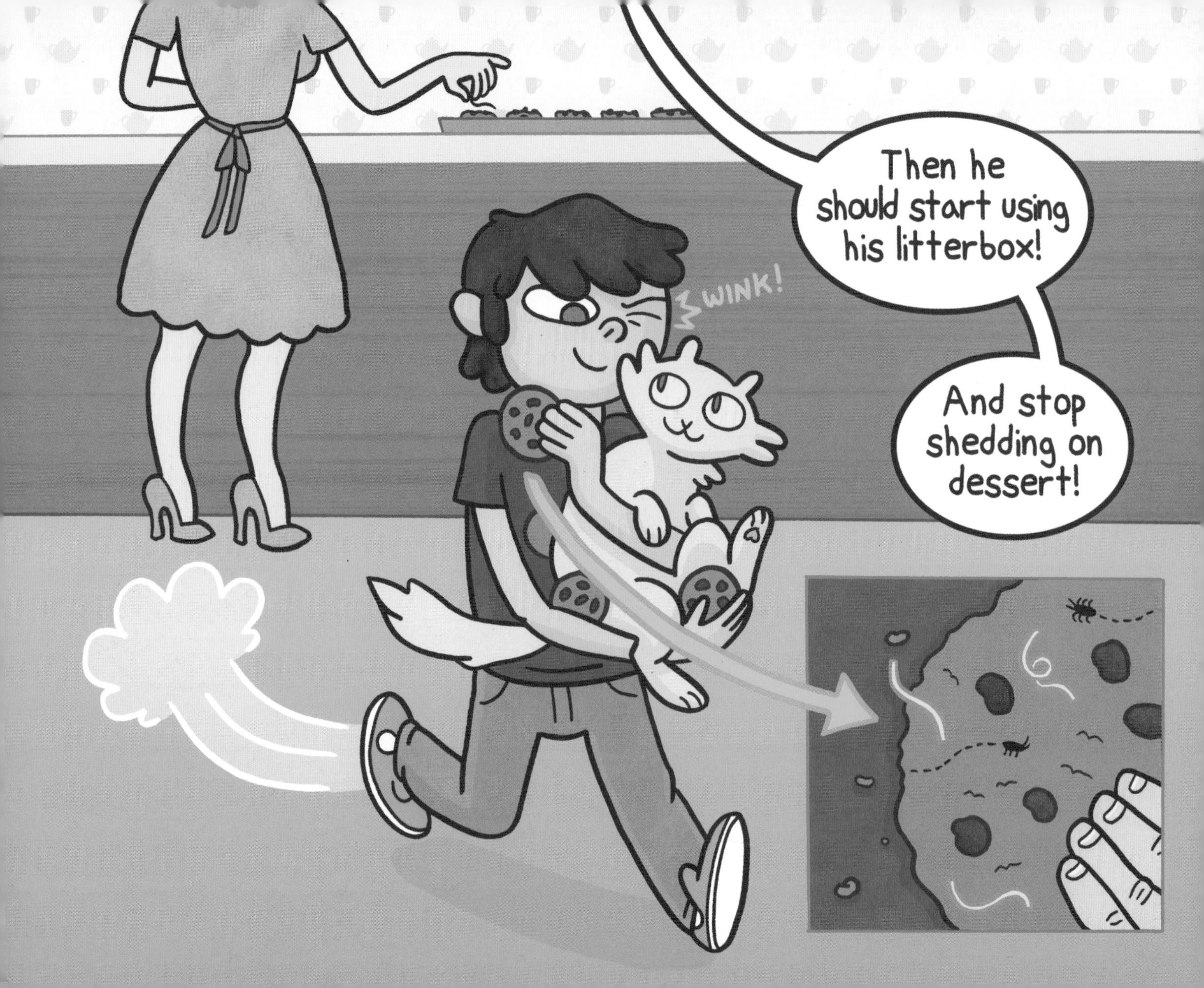
Then he should start using his litterbox!
WINK!
And stop shedding on dessert!

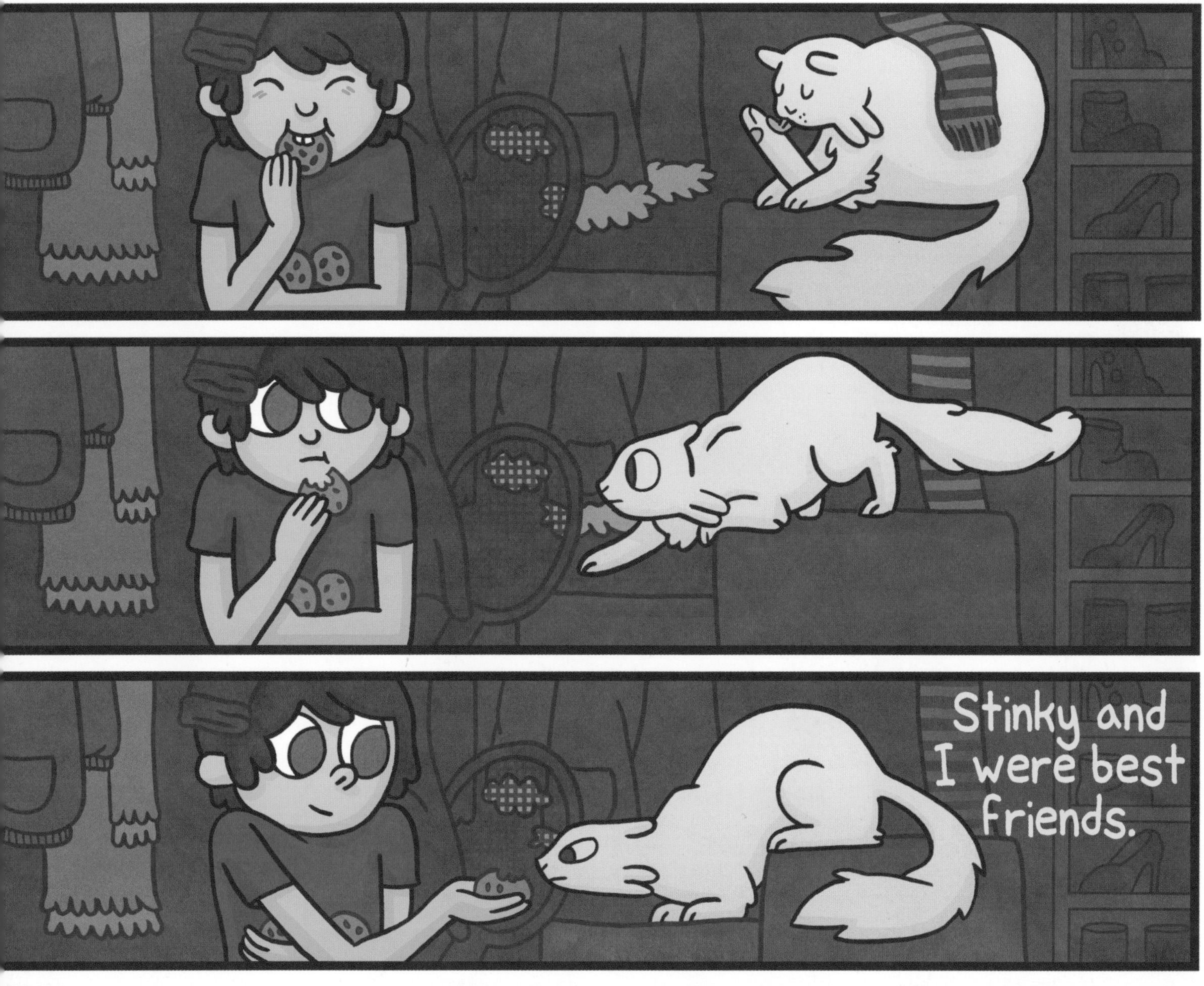
Stinky and I were best friends.

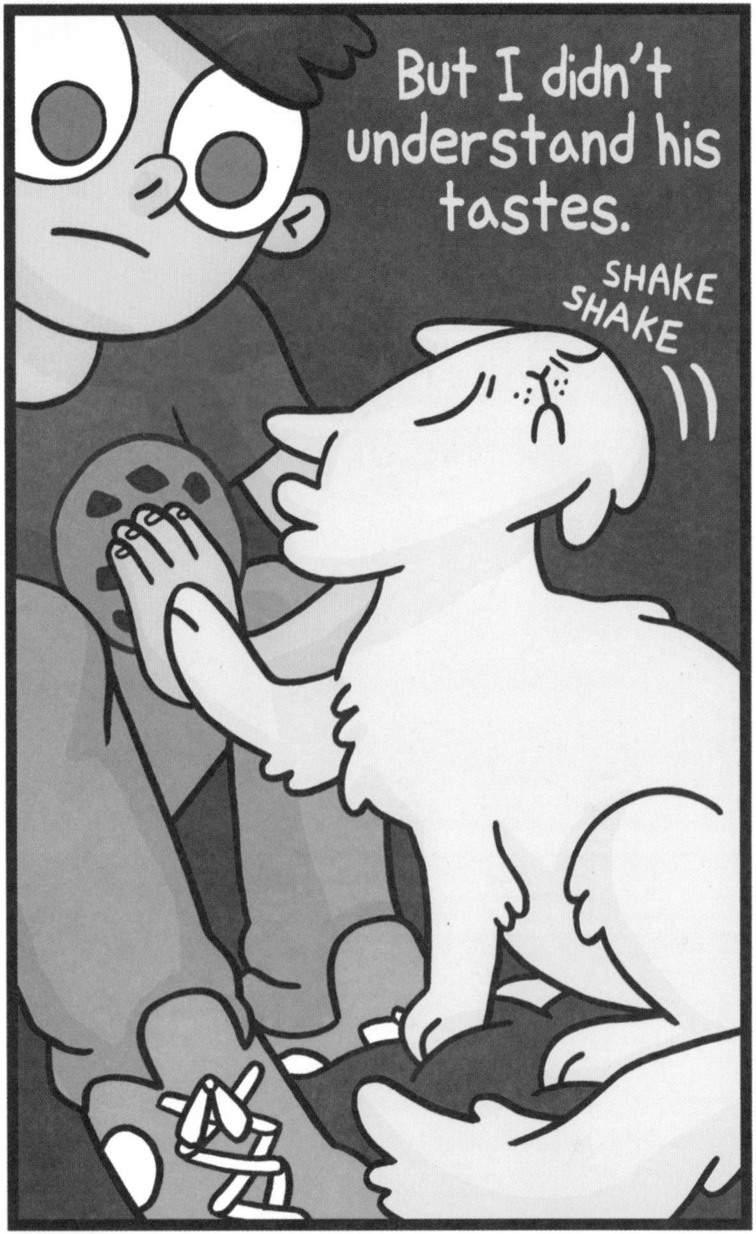
But I didn't understand his tastes.
SHAKE
SHAKE

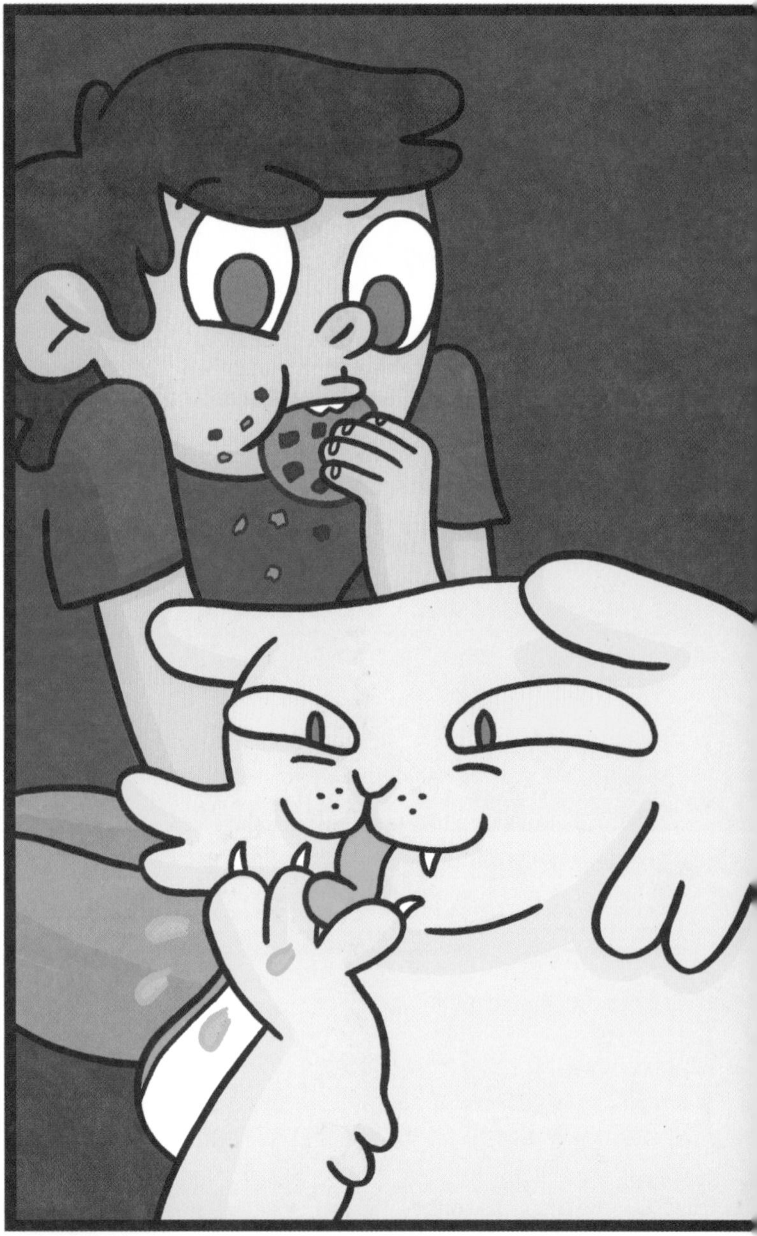

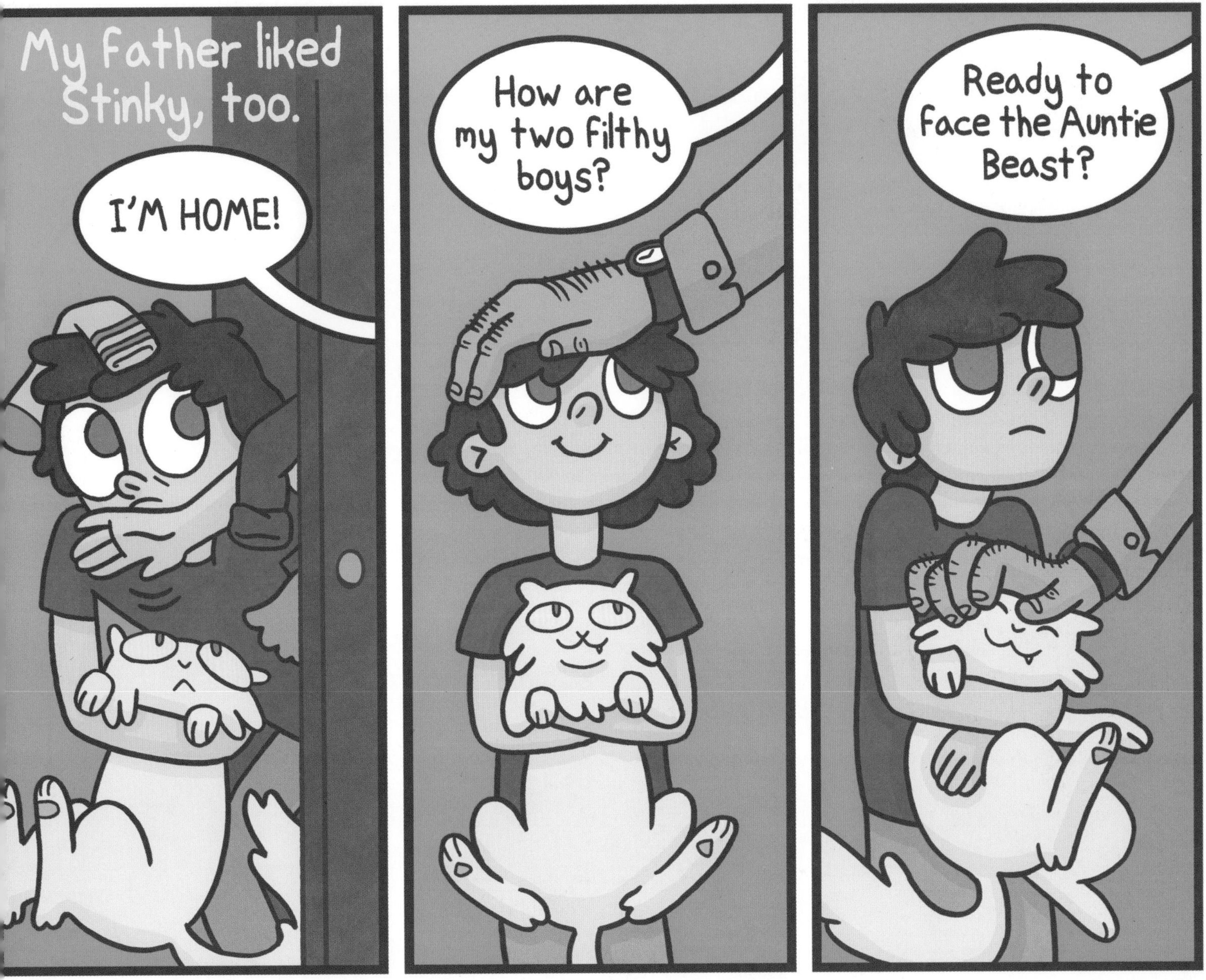
My father liked Stinky, too.
I'M HOME!
How are my two filthy boys?
Ready to face the Auntie Beast?

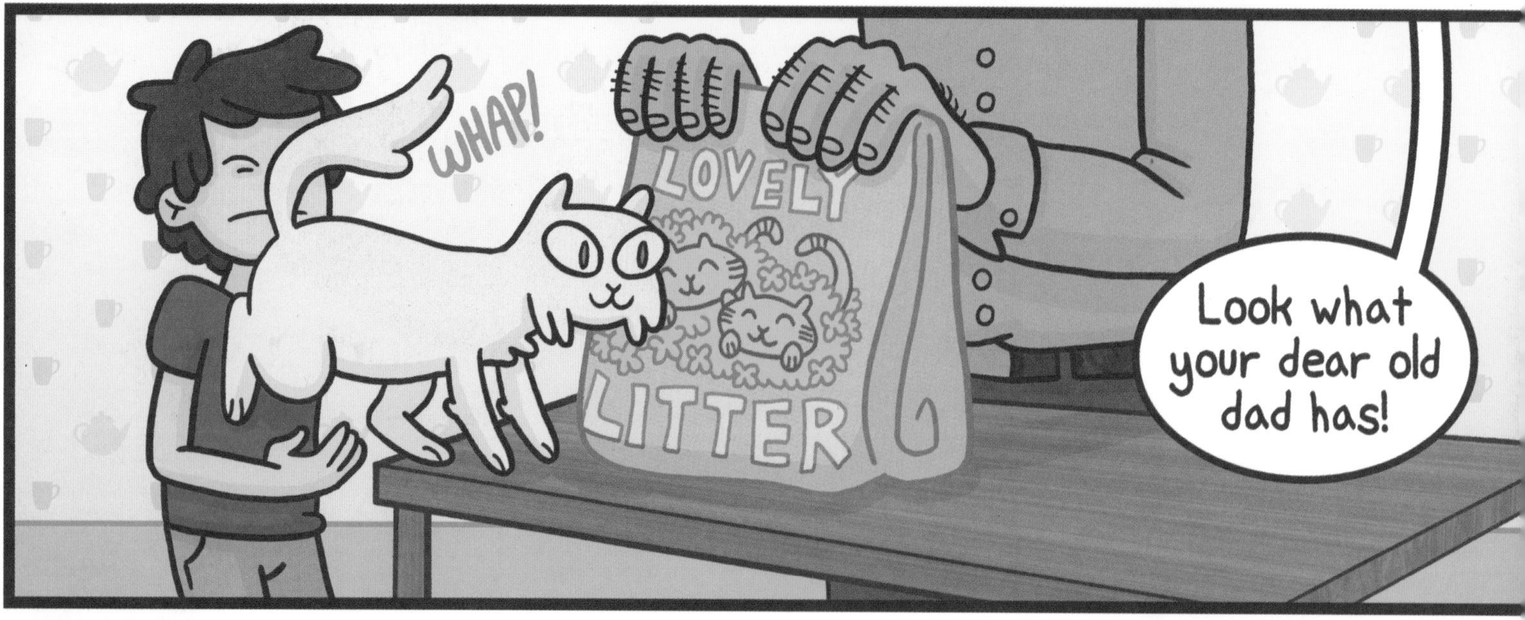
WHAP!
LOVELY LITTER
Look what your dear old dad has!

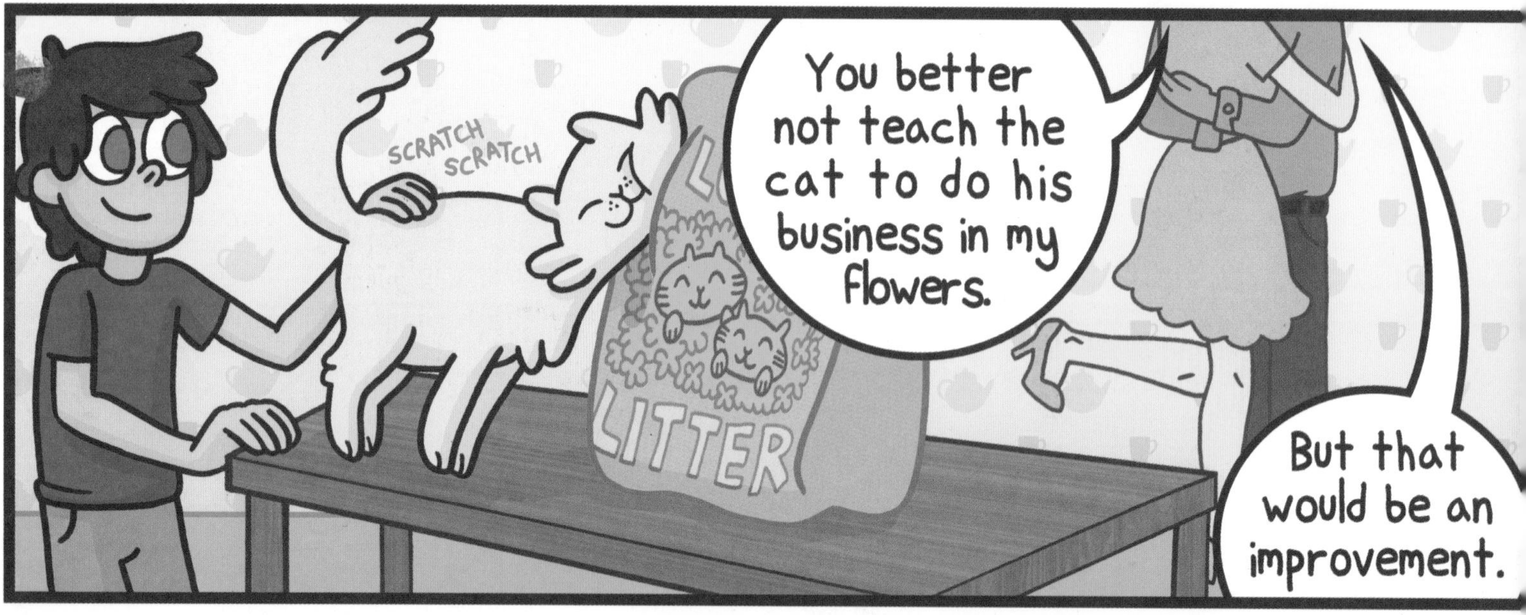
SCRATCH SCRATCH
You better not teach the cat to do his business in my flowers.
LITTER
But that would be an improvement.

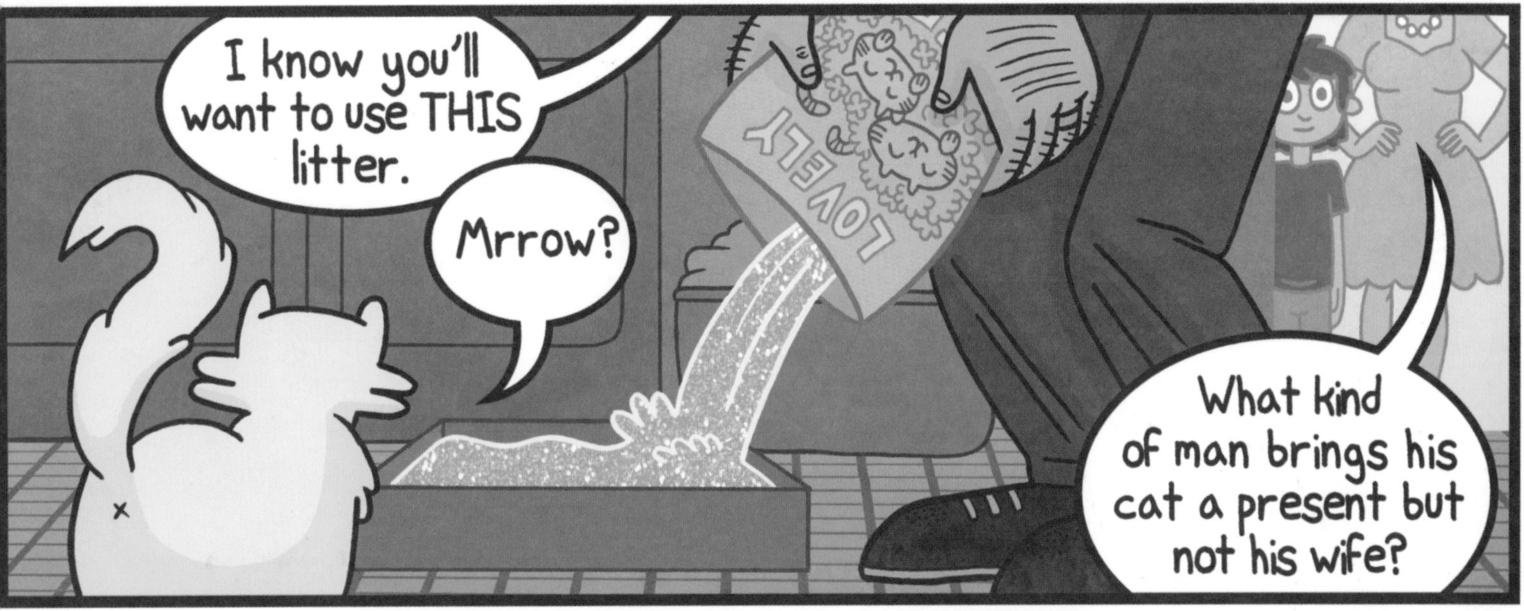
I know you'll want to use THIS litter.
Mrrow?
LOVELY
What kind of man brings his cat a present but not his wife?
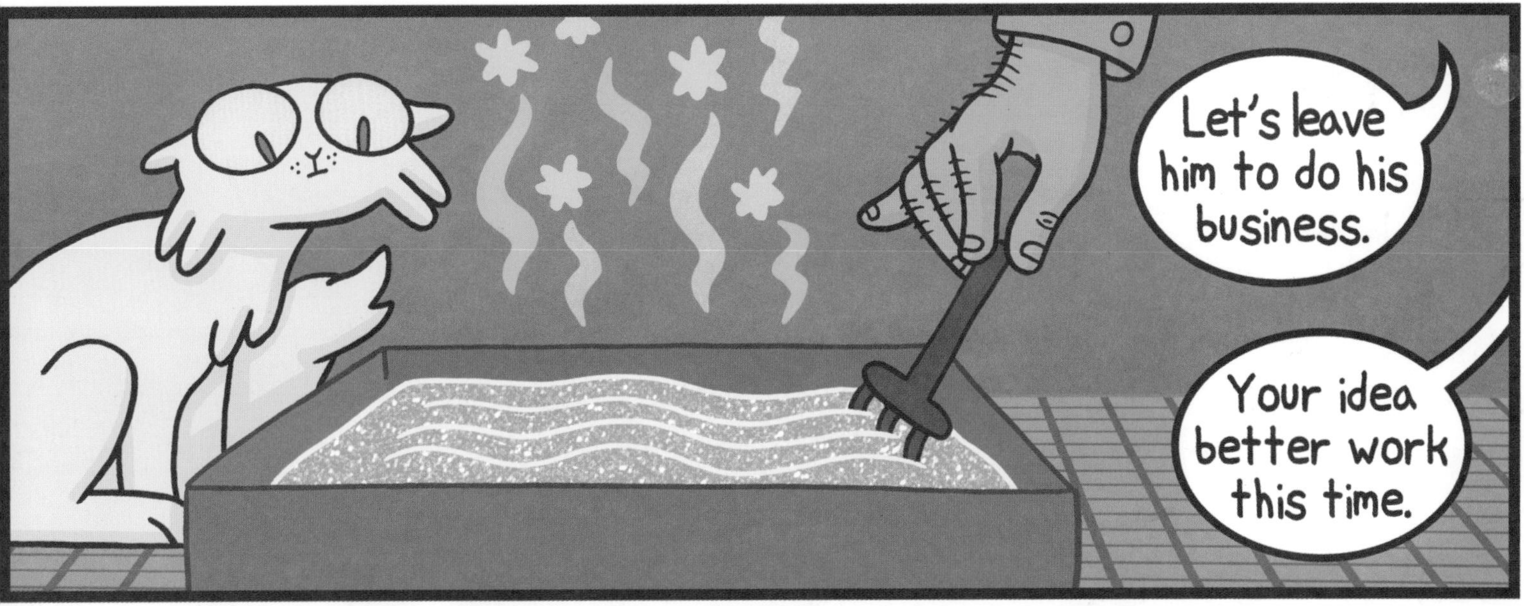
Let's leave him to do his business.
Your idea better work this time.

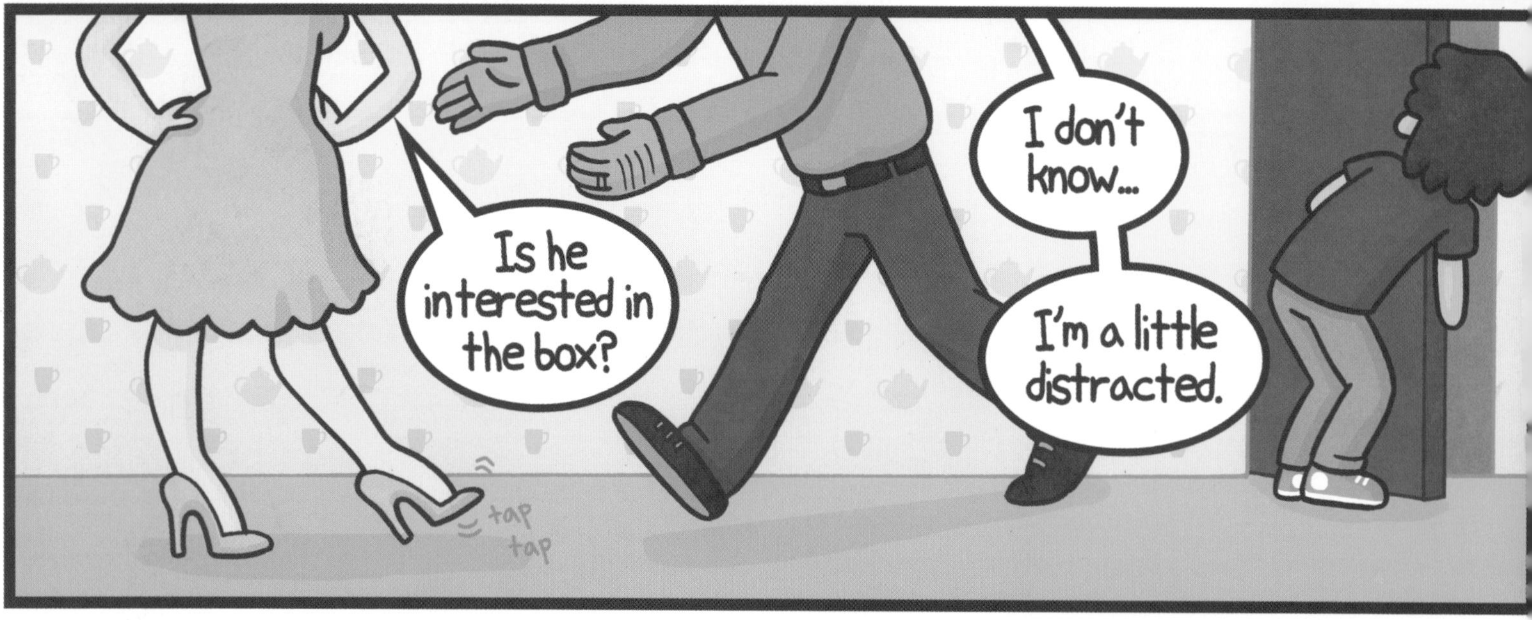
Is he interested in the box?
I don't know...
I'm a little distracted.
tap tap
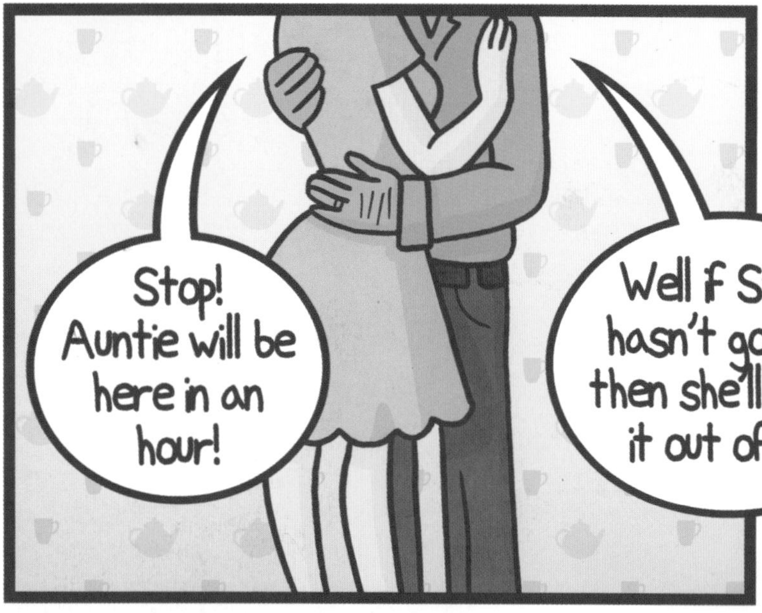
Stop! Auntie will be here in an hour!
Well if Stinky hasn't gone by then she'll scare it out of him.
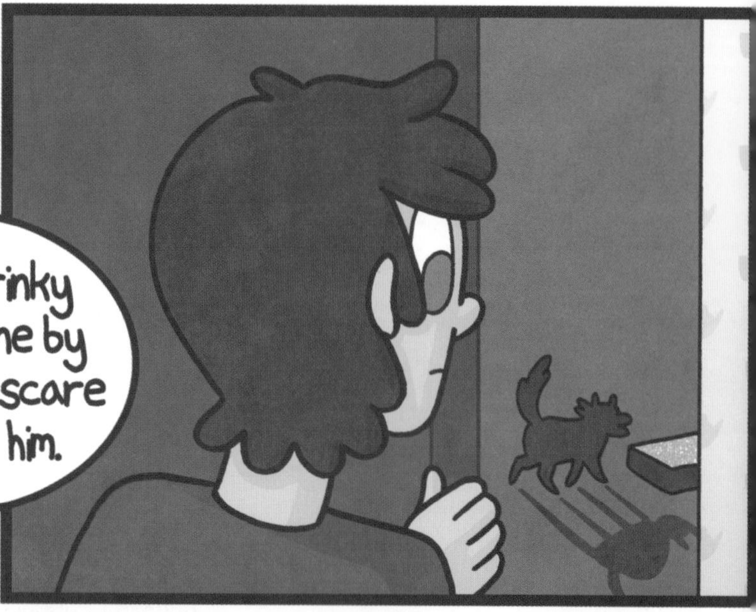

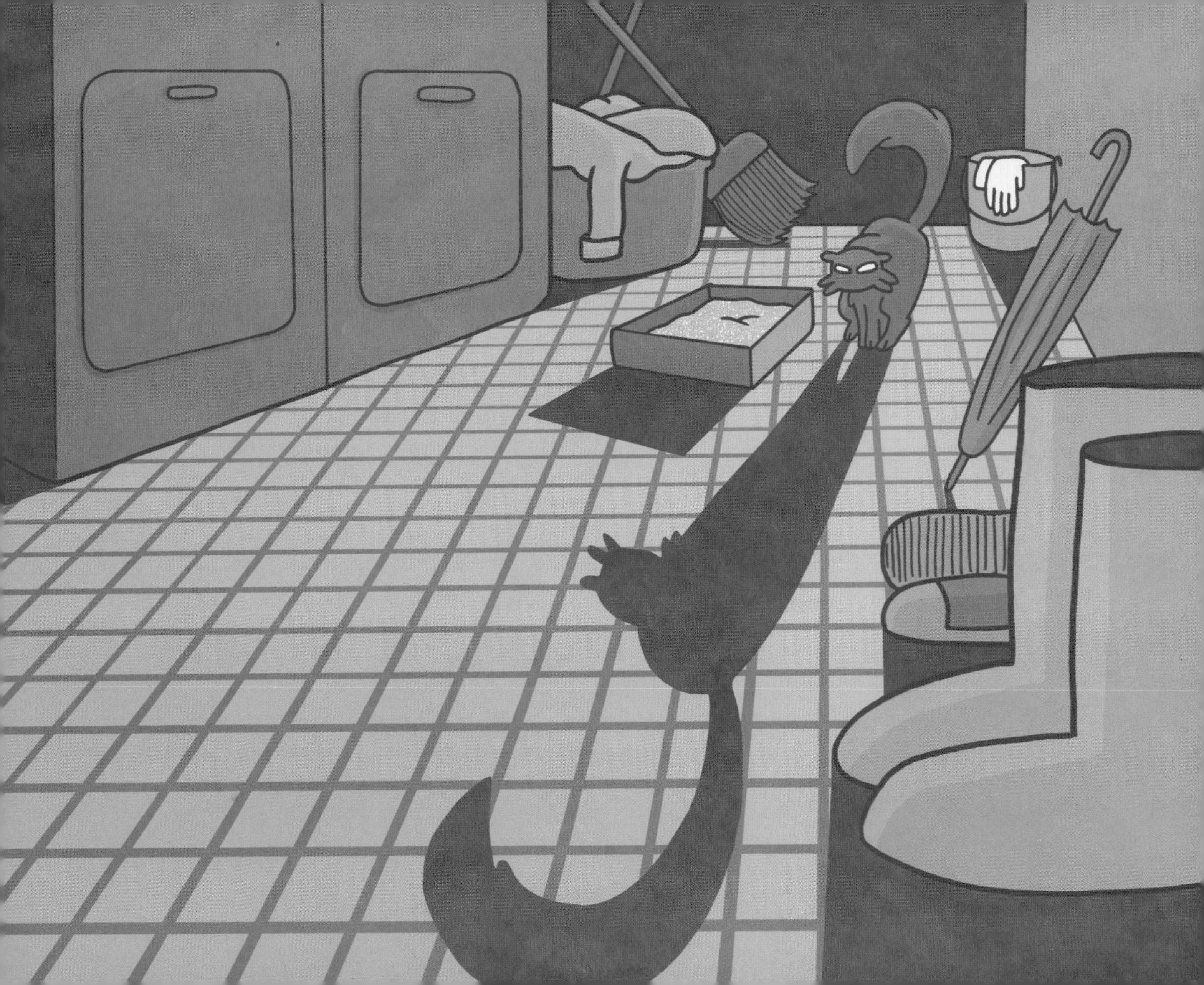

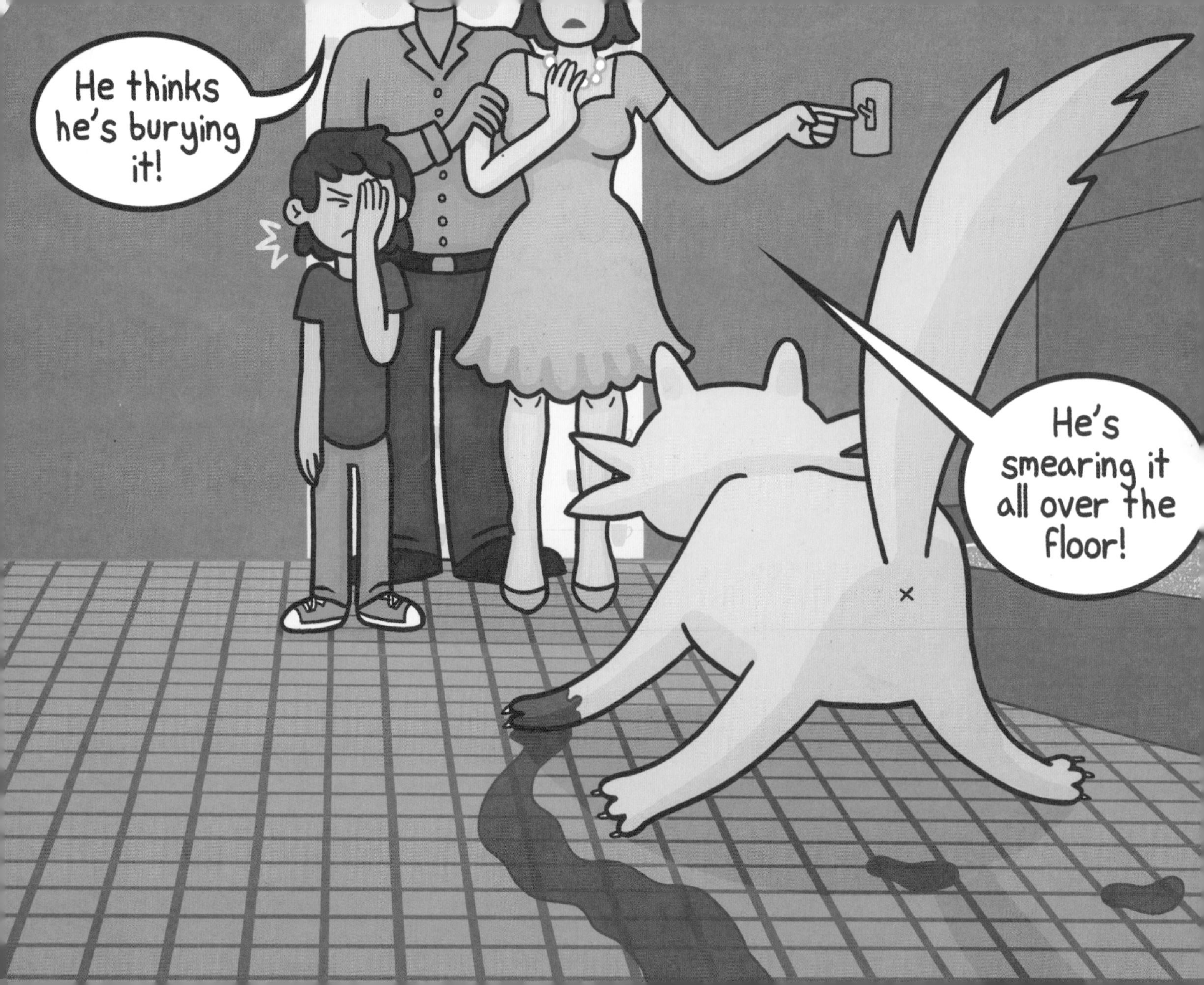
He thinks he's burying it!
He's smearing it all over the floor!

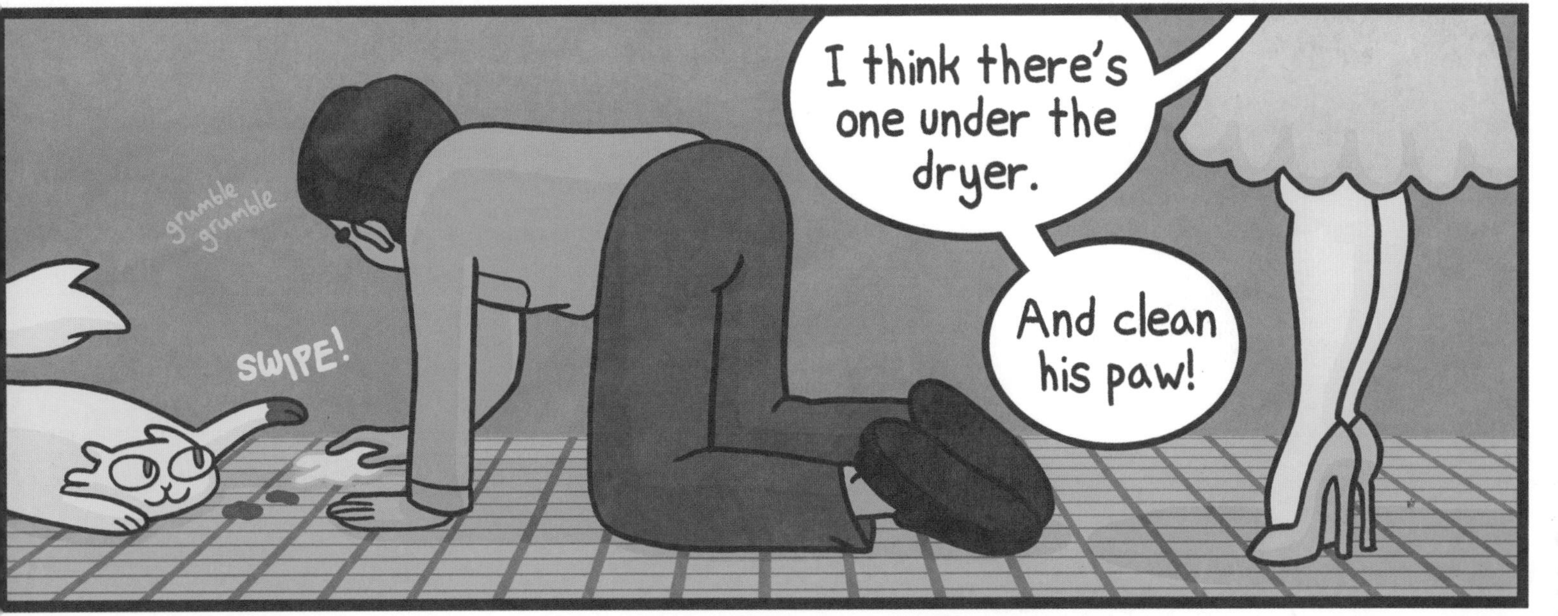
I think there's one under the dryer.
And clean his paw!
grumble grumble
SWIPE!

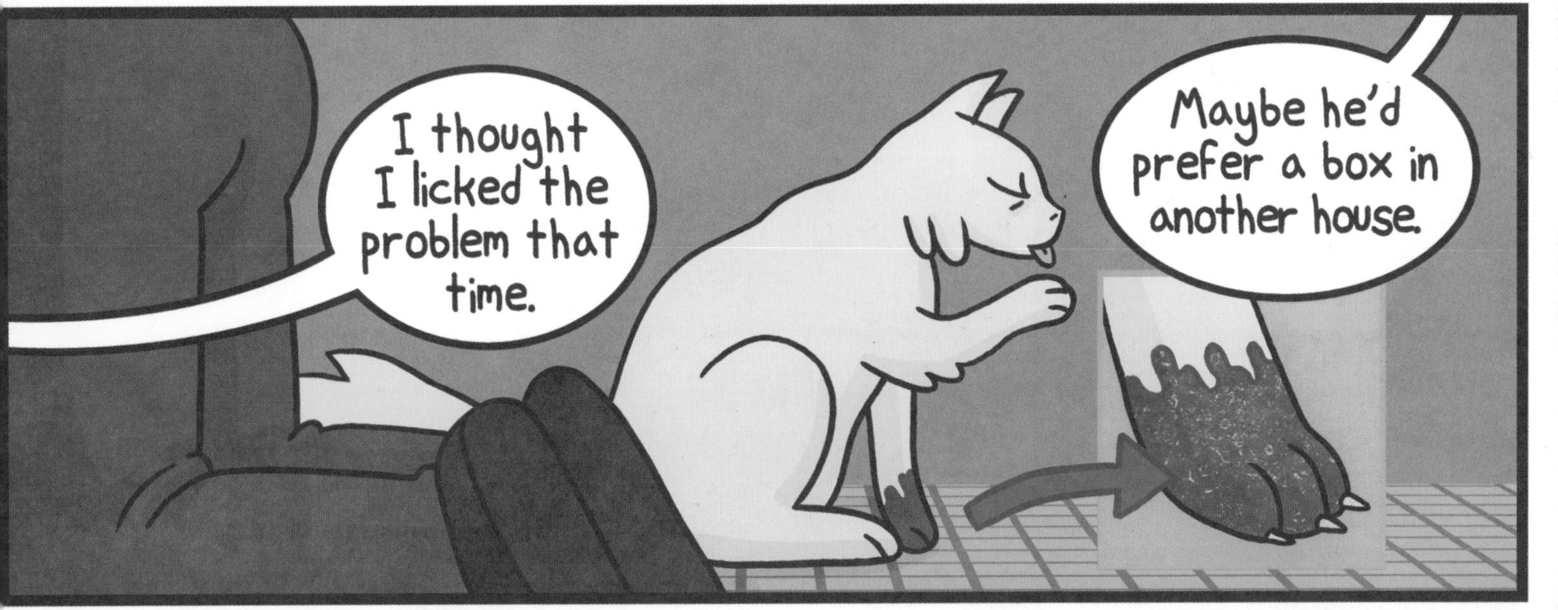
I thought I licked the problem that time.
Maybe he'd prefer a box in another house.

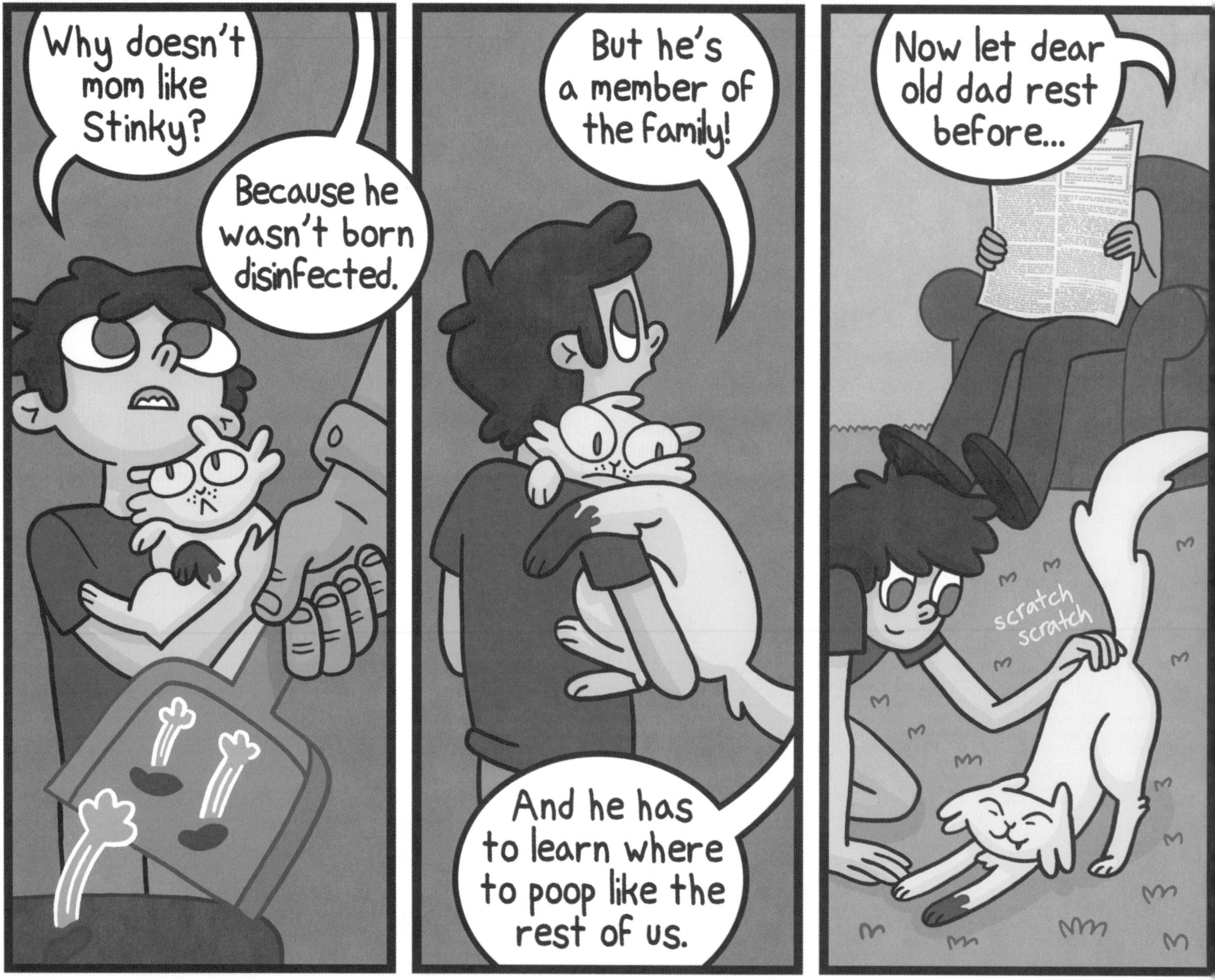
Why doesn't mom like Stinky?
Because he wasn't born disinfected.
But he's a member of the family!
And he has to learn where to poop like the rest of us.
Now let dear old dad rest before...
scratch scratch

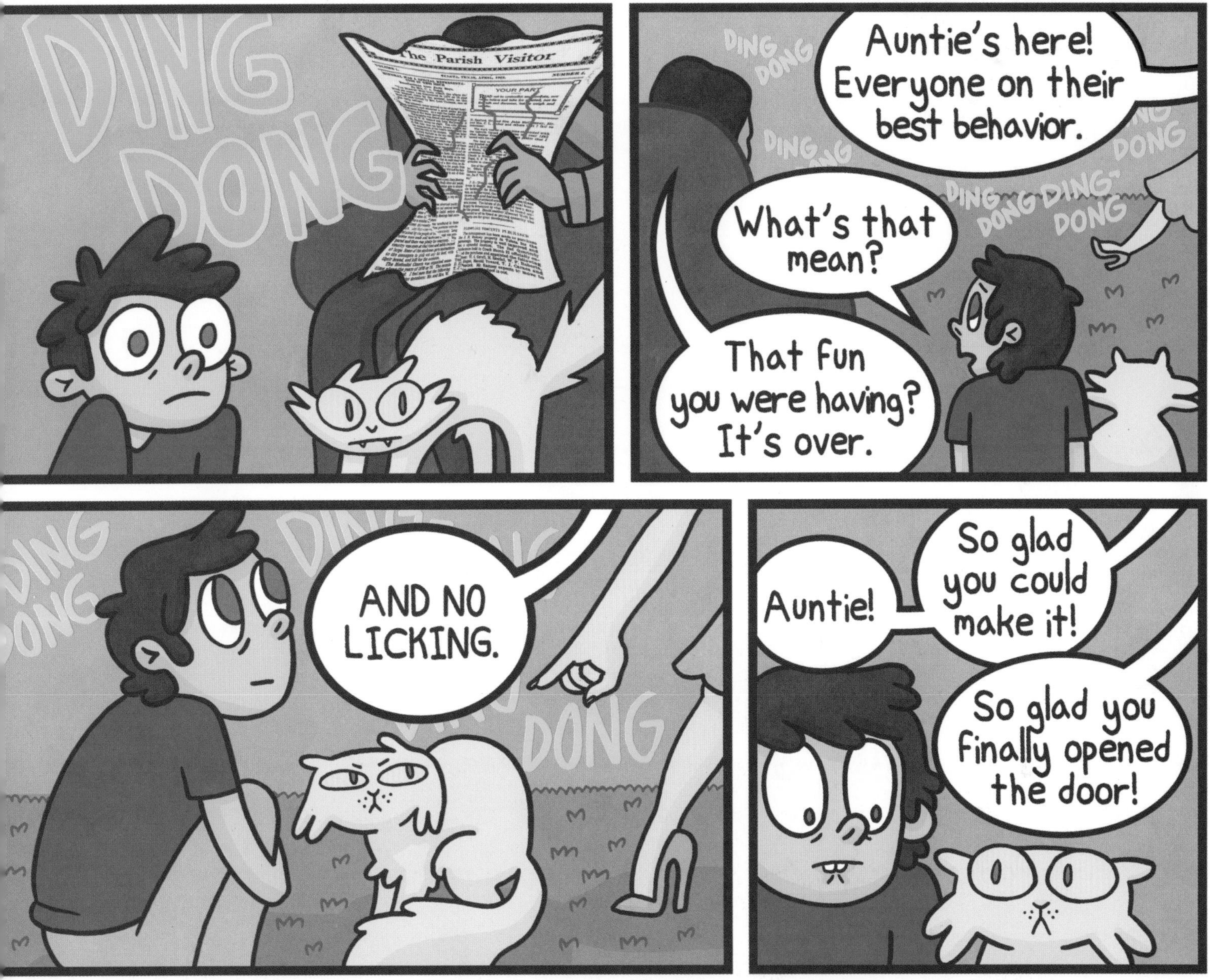
DING DONG
The Parish Visitor
YOUR PART
DING DONG
Auntie's here! Everyone on their best behavior.
DING DONG
DONG
DING DONG DING-DONG
What's that mean?
That fun you were having? It's over.
DING DONG
DONG
AND NO LICKING.
DONG
Auntie!
So glad you could make it!
So glad you finally opened the door!

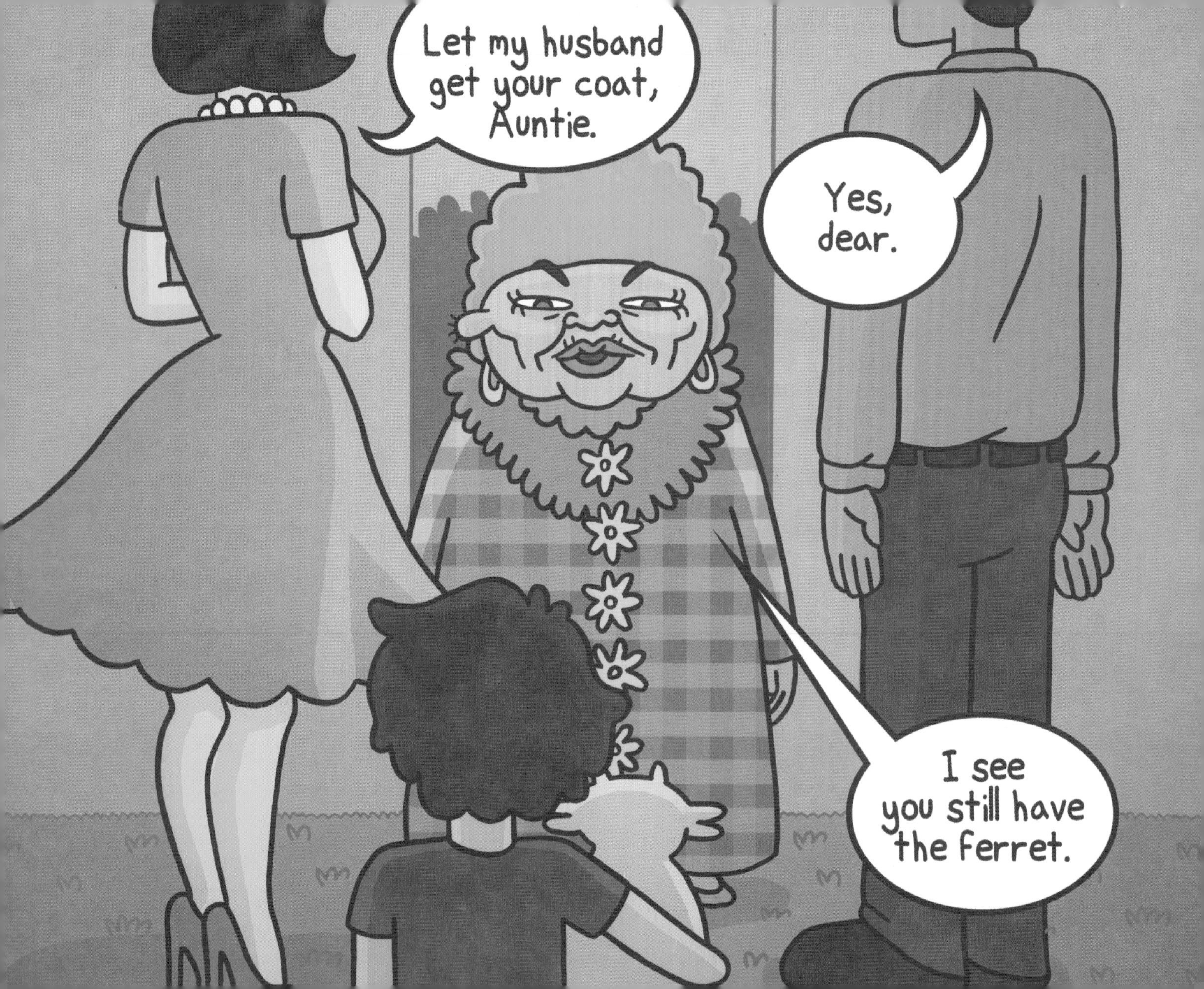
Let my husband get your coat, Auntie.
Yes, dear.
I see you still have the ferret.

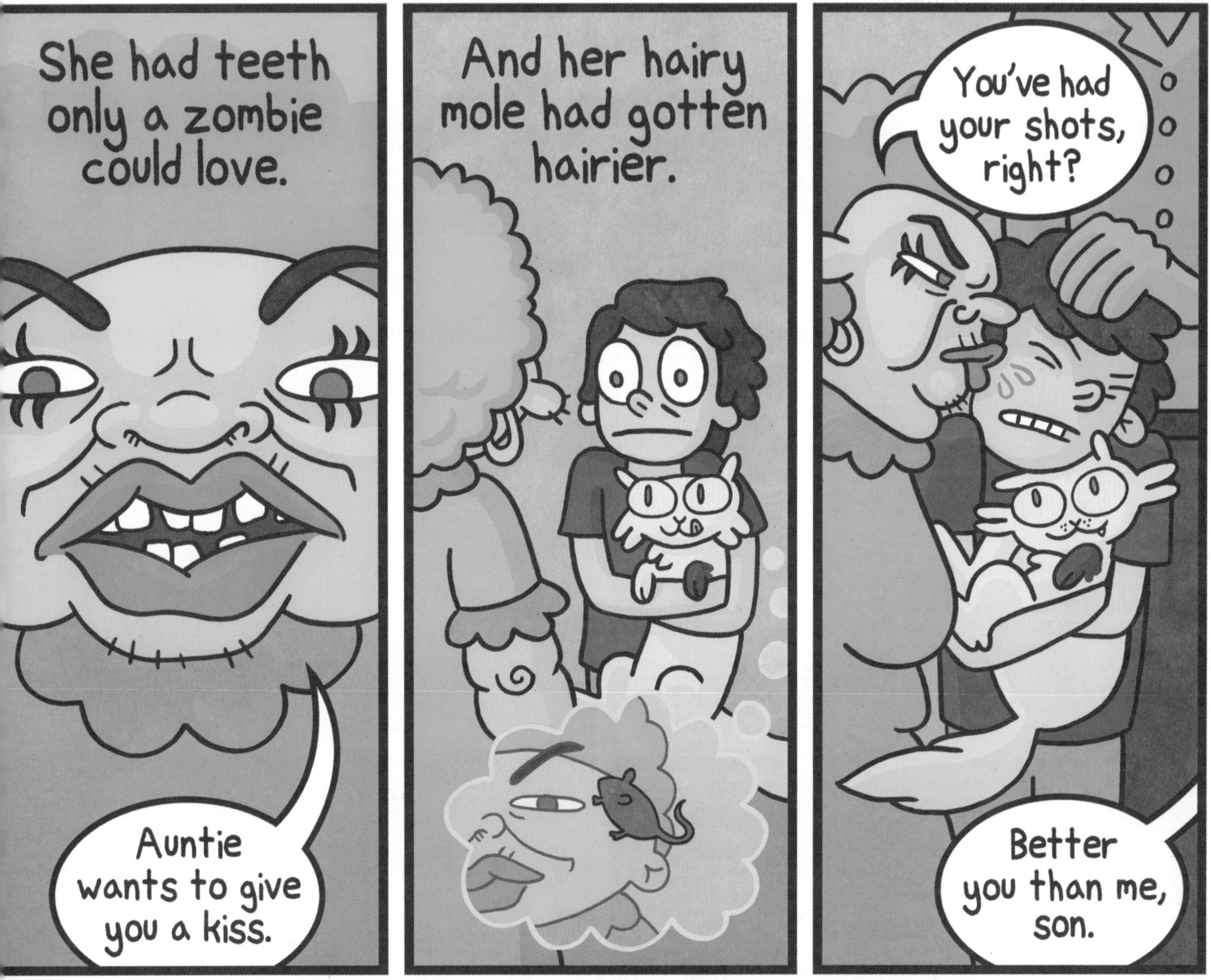
She had teeth only a zombie could love.
Auntie wants to give you a kiss.
And her hairy mole had gotten hairier.
You've had your shots, right?
Better you than me, son.

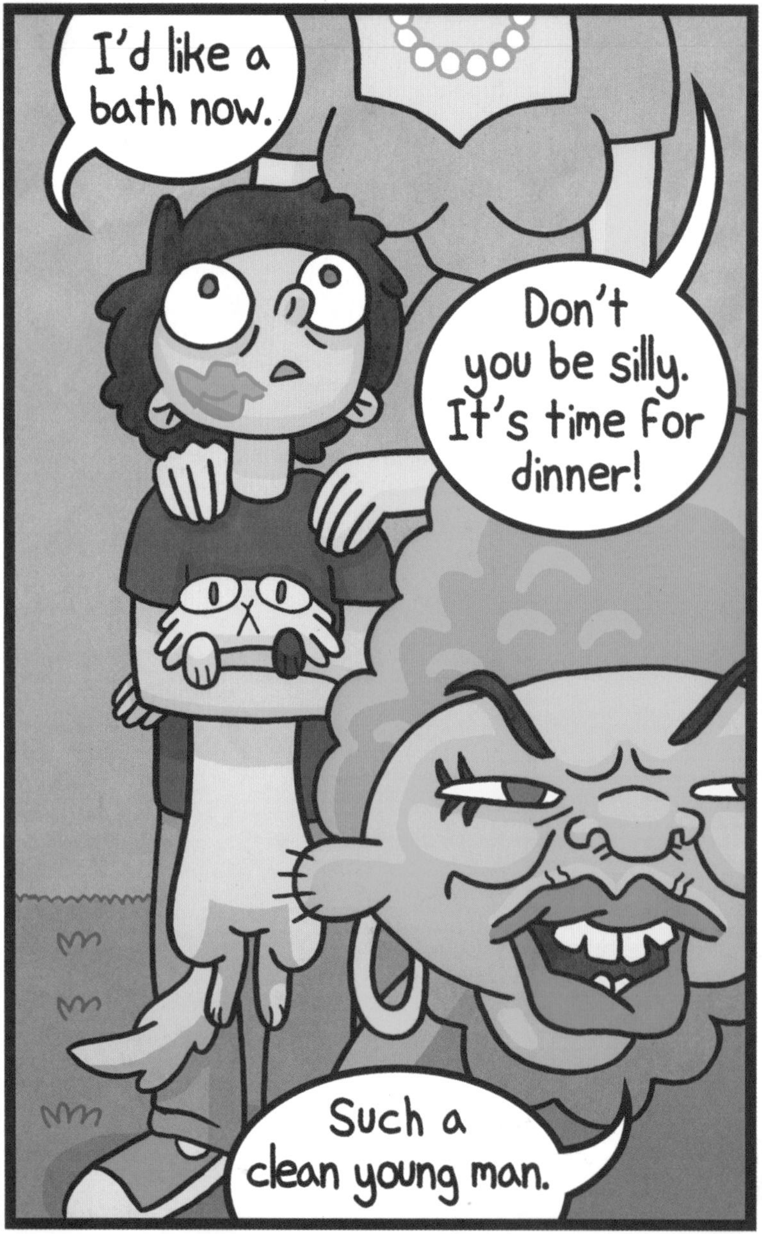

I'd like a bath now.
Don't you be silly. It's time for dinner!
Such a clean young man.

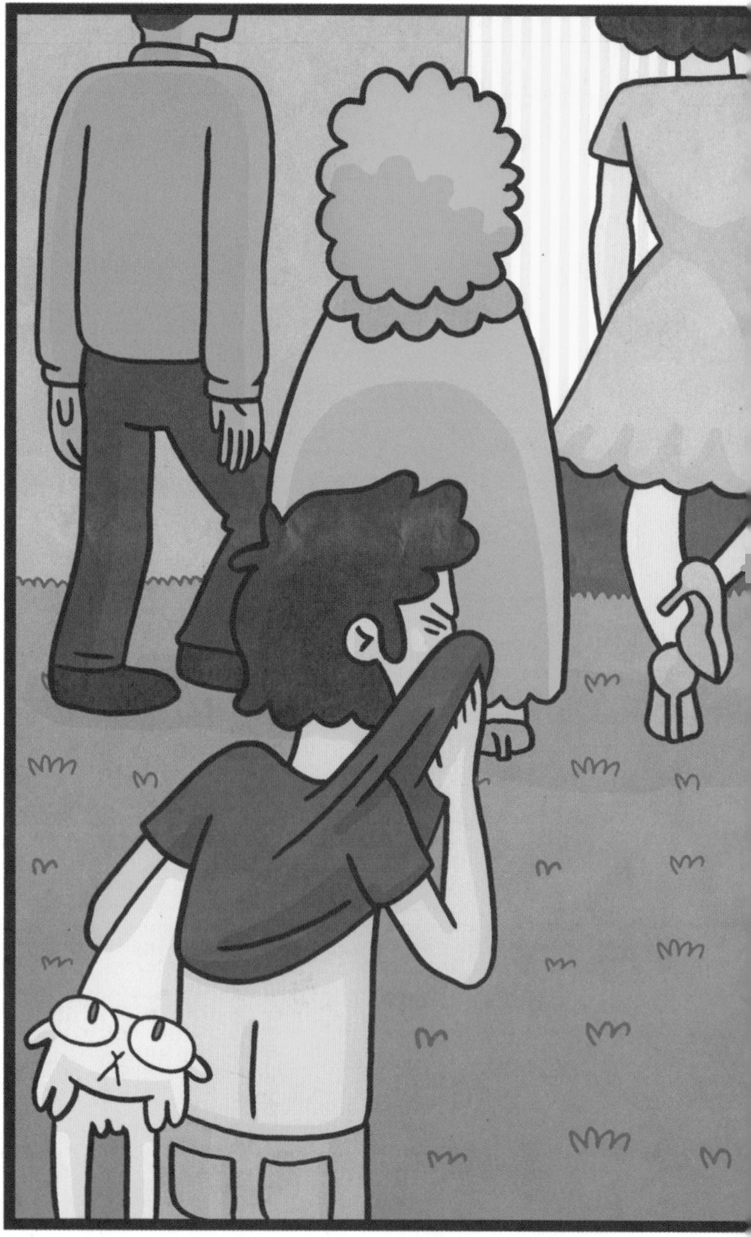

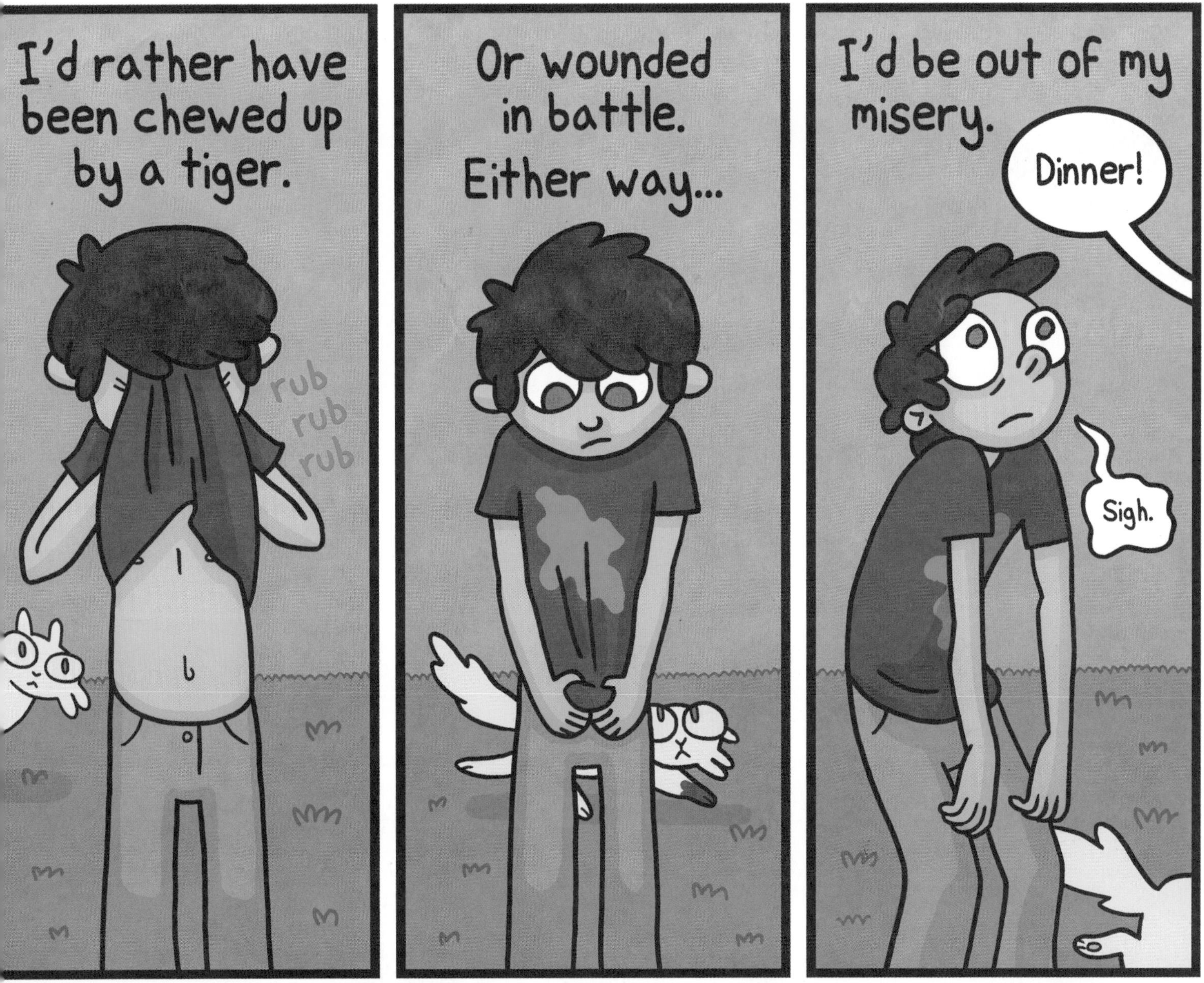

I'd rather have been chewed up by a tiger.
rub rub rub
Or wounded in battle. Either way...
I'd be out of my misery.
Dinner!
Sigh.

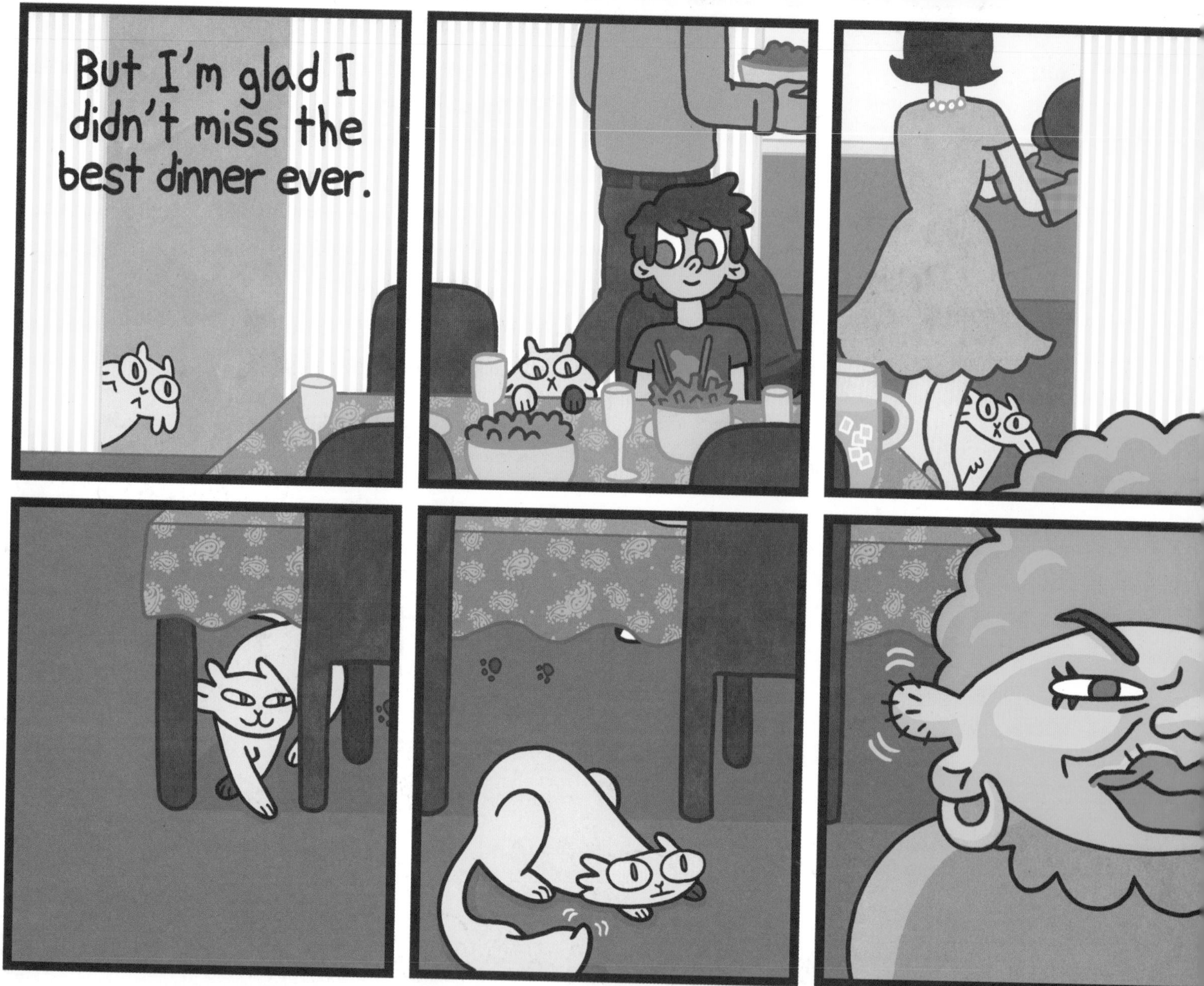
But I'm glad I didn't miss the best dinner ever.

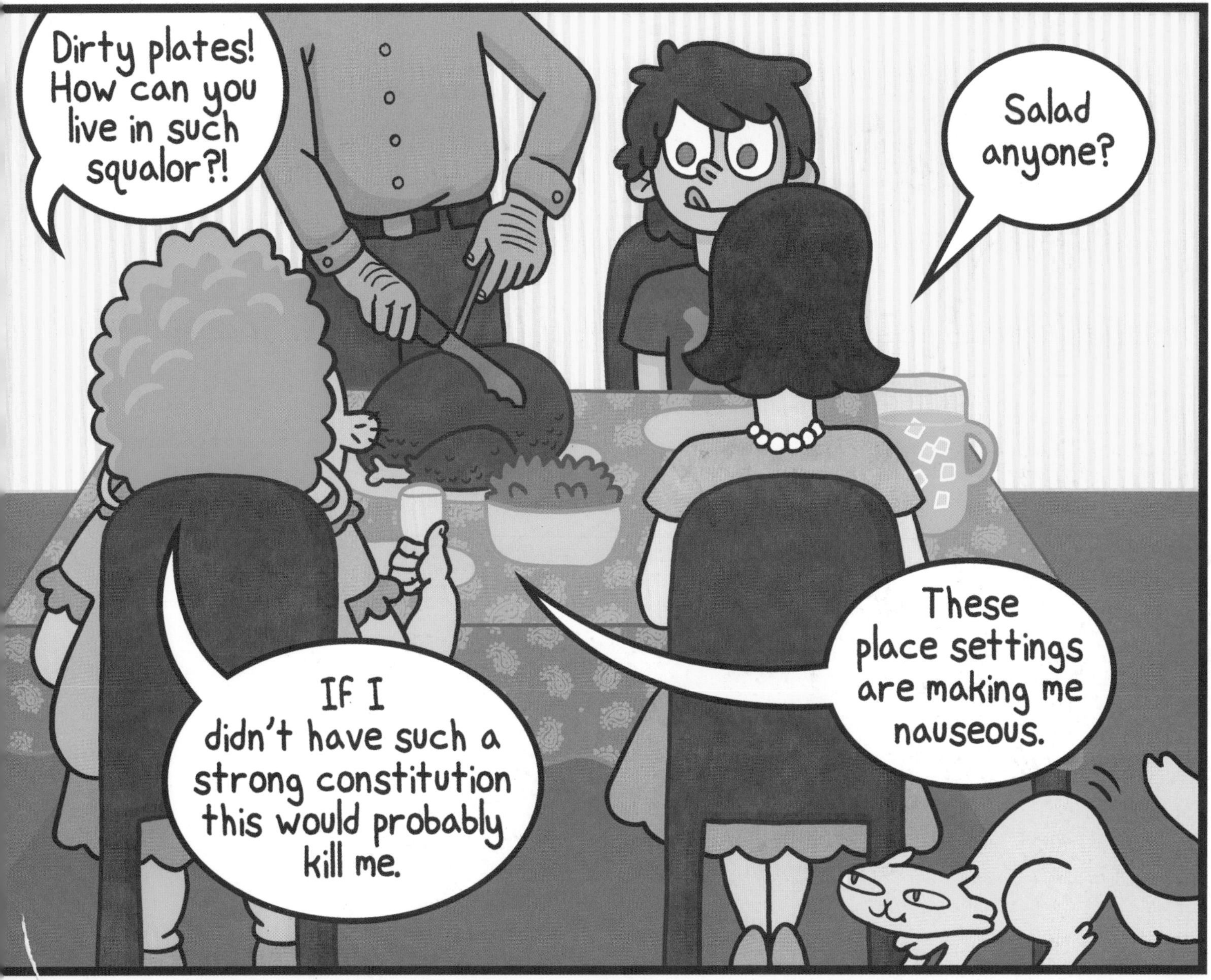
Dirty plates! How can you live in such squalor?!
Salad anyone?
If I didn't have such a strong constitution this would probably kill me.
These place settings are making me nauseous.

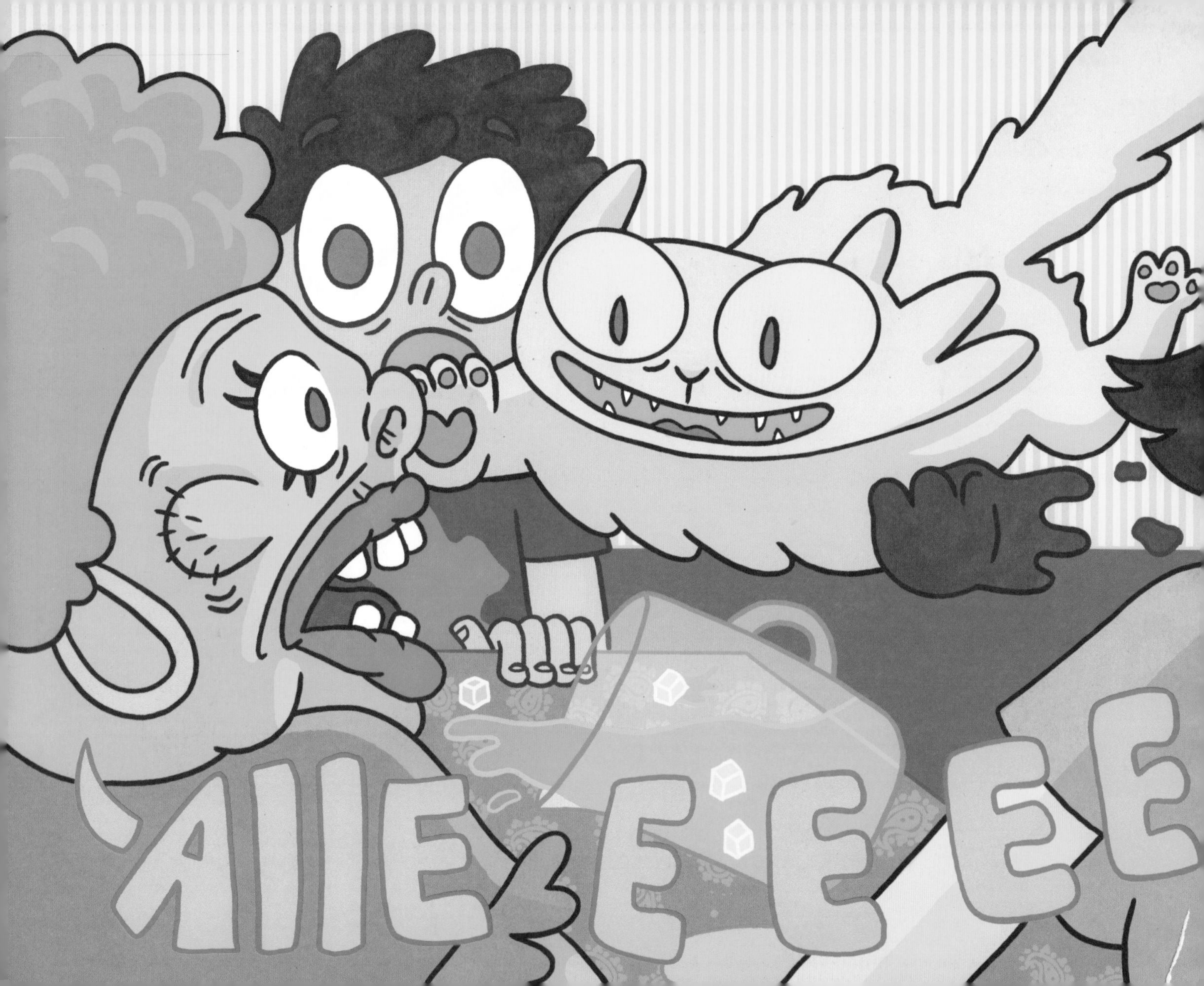

AIIEEEEE

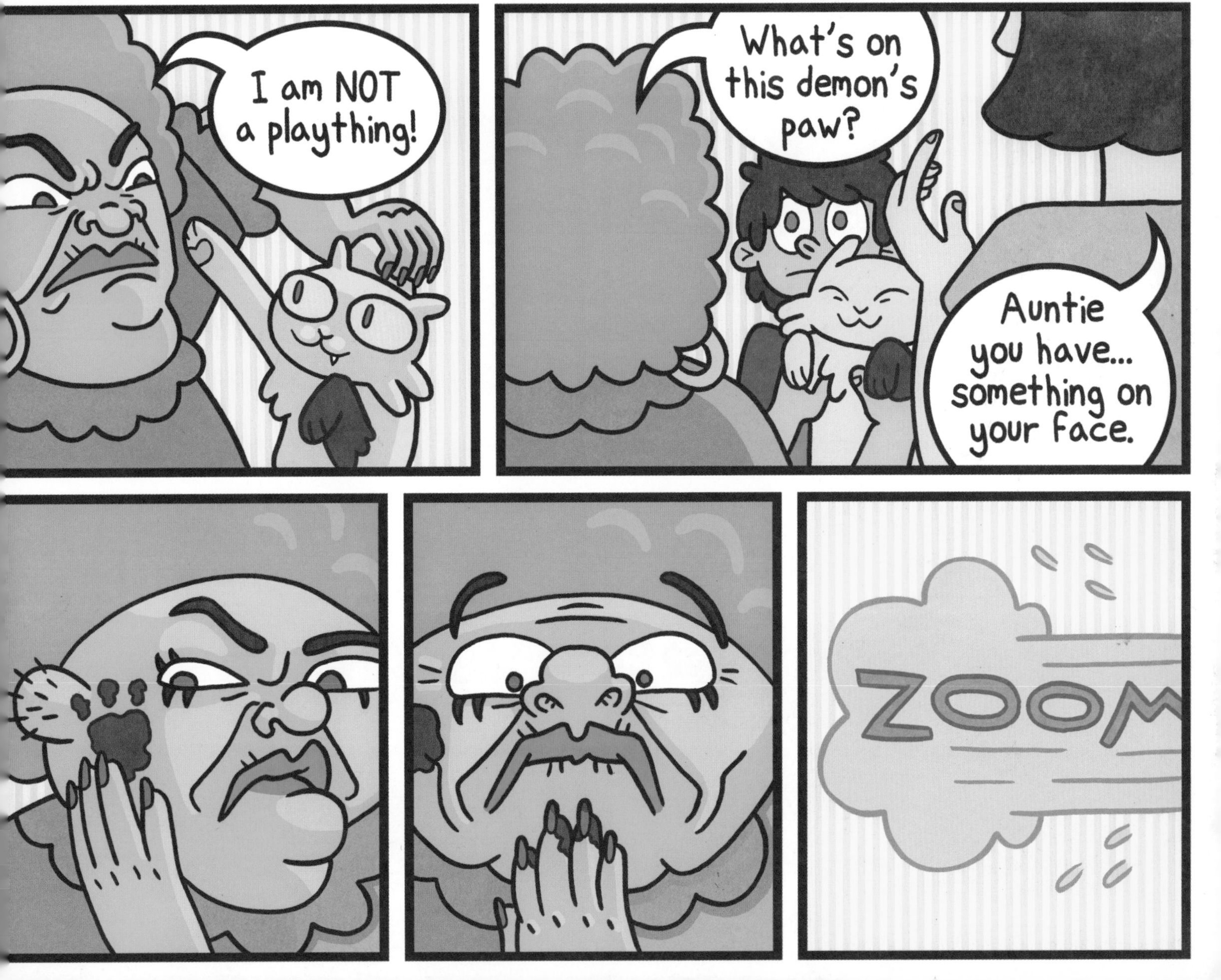
I am NOT a plaything!
What's on this demon's paw?
Auntie you have... something on your face.
ZOOM

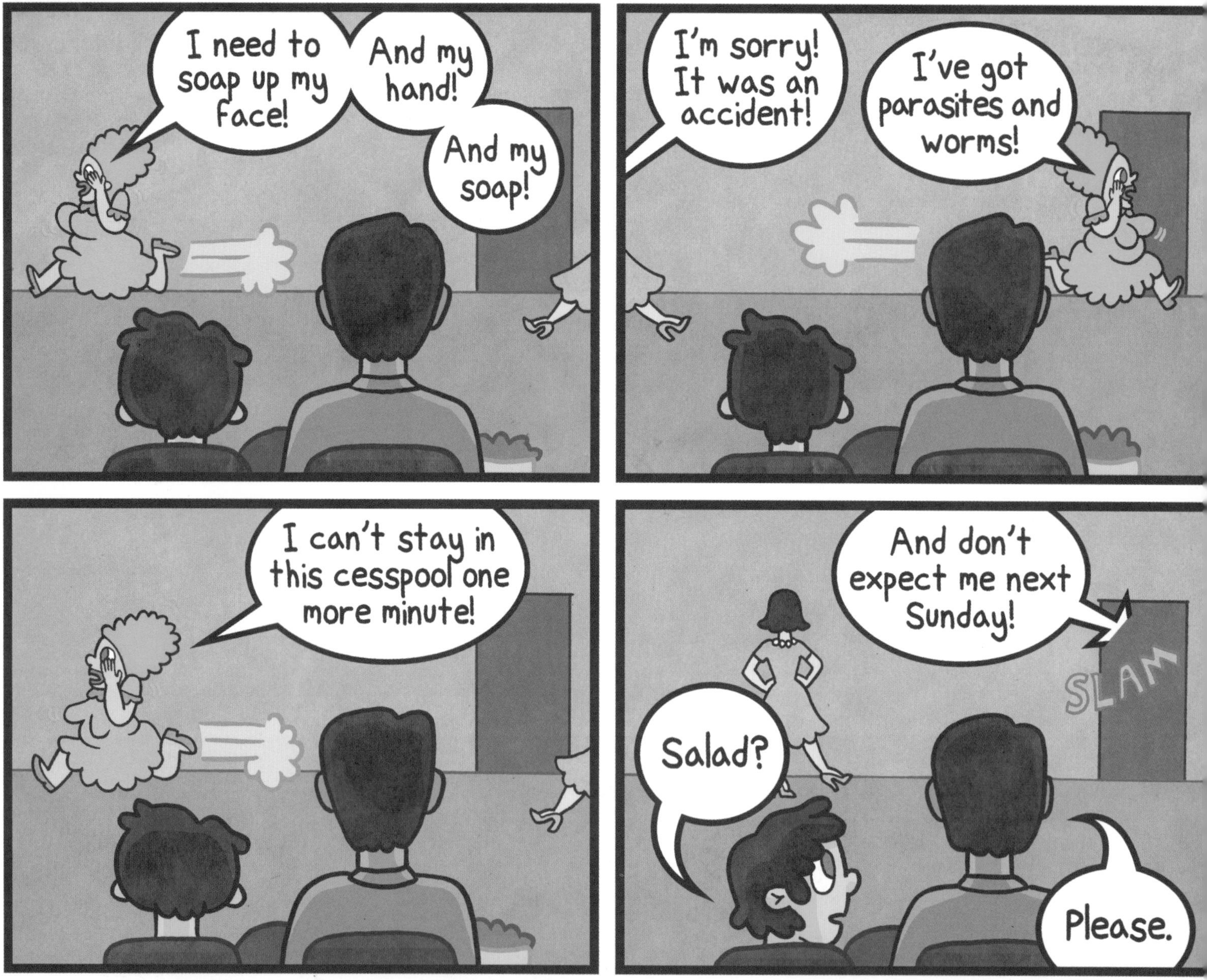
I need to soap up my face!
And my hand!
And my soap!
I'm sorry! It was an accident!
I've got parasites and worms!
I can't stay in this cesspool one more minute!
And don't expect me next Sunday!
SLAM
Salad?
Please.

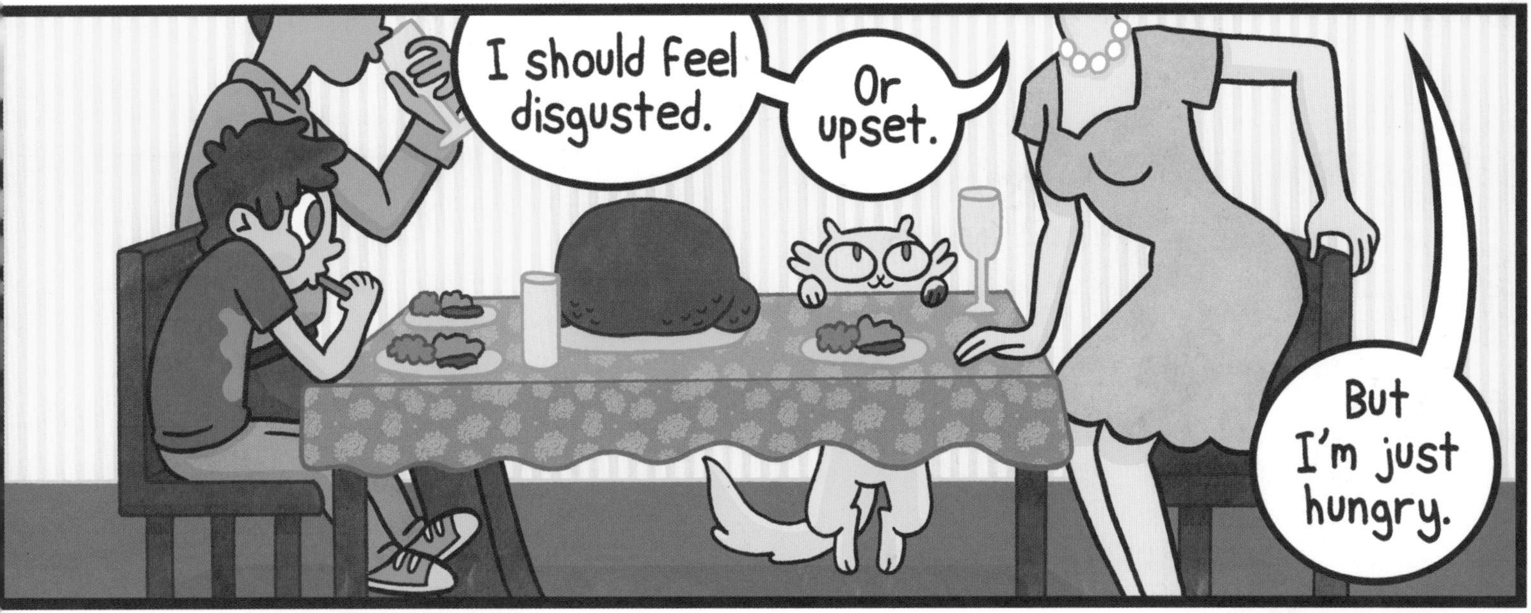
I should feel disgusted.
Or upset.
But I'm just hungry.

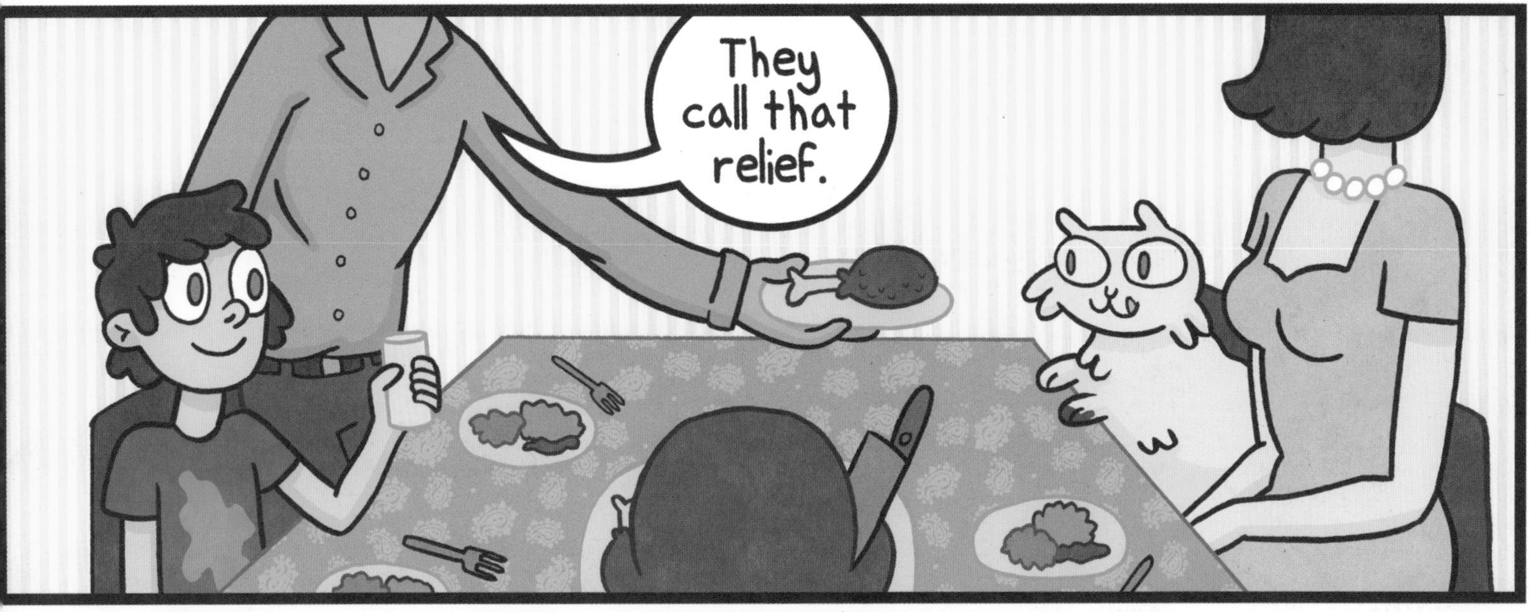
They call that relief.

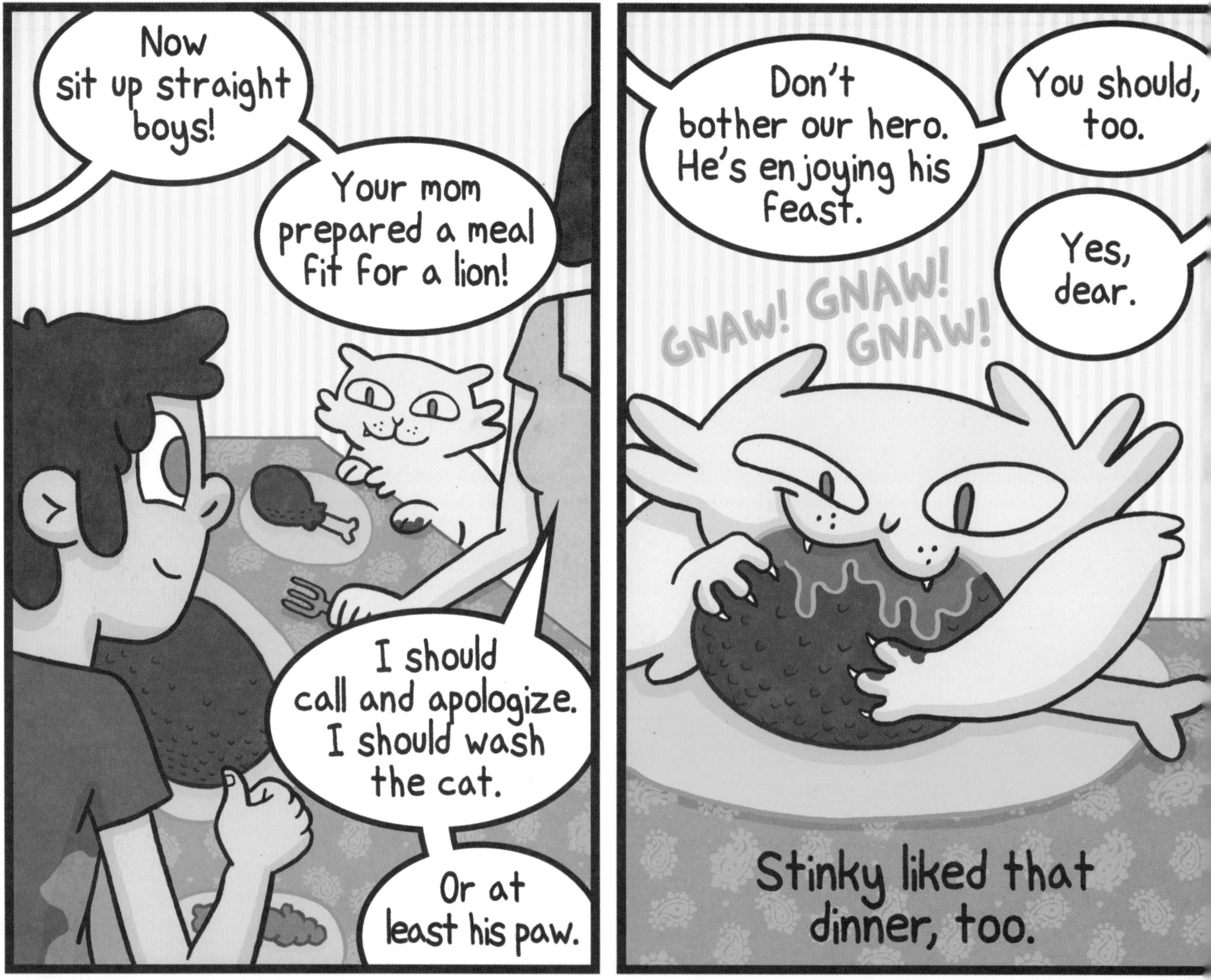
Now sit up straight boys!
Your mom prepared a meal fit for a lion!
I should call and apologize. I should wash the cat.
Or at least his paw.
Don't bother our hero. He's enjoying his feast.
You should, too.
Yes, dear.
GNAW! GNAW! GNAW!
Stinky liked that dinner, too.

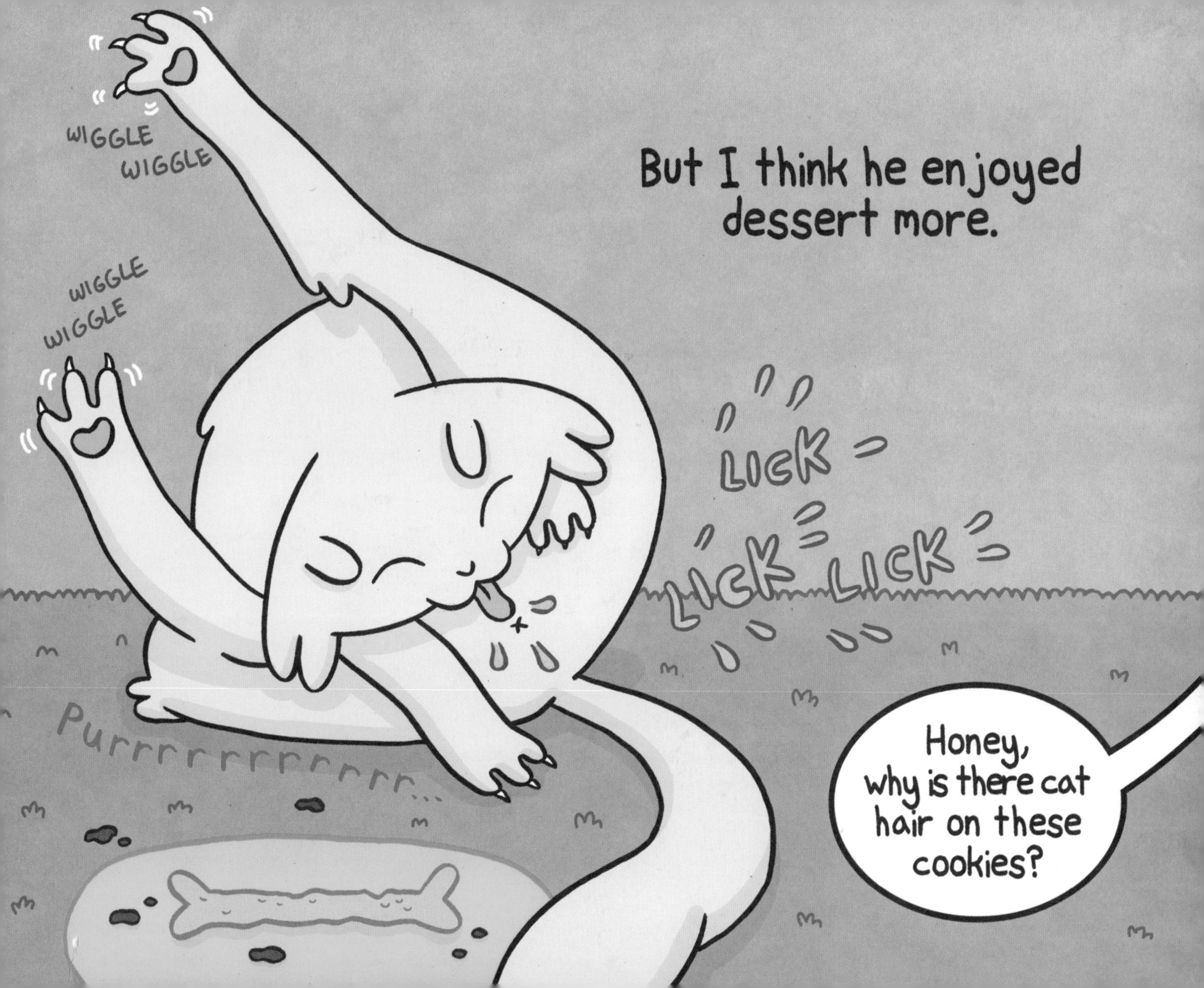
But I think he enjoyed dessert more.
WIGGLE WIGGLE
WIGGLE WIGGLE
LICK
LICK LICK
Purrrrrrrrrrrr...
Honey, why is there cat hair on these cookies?

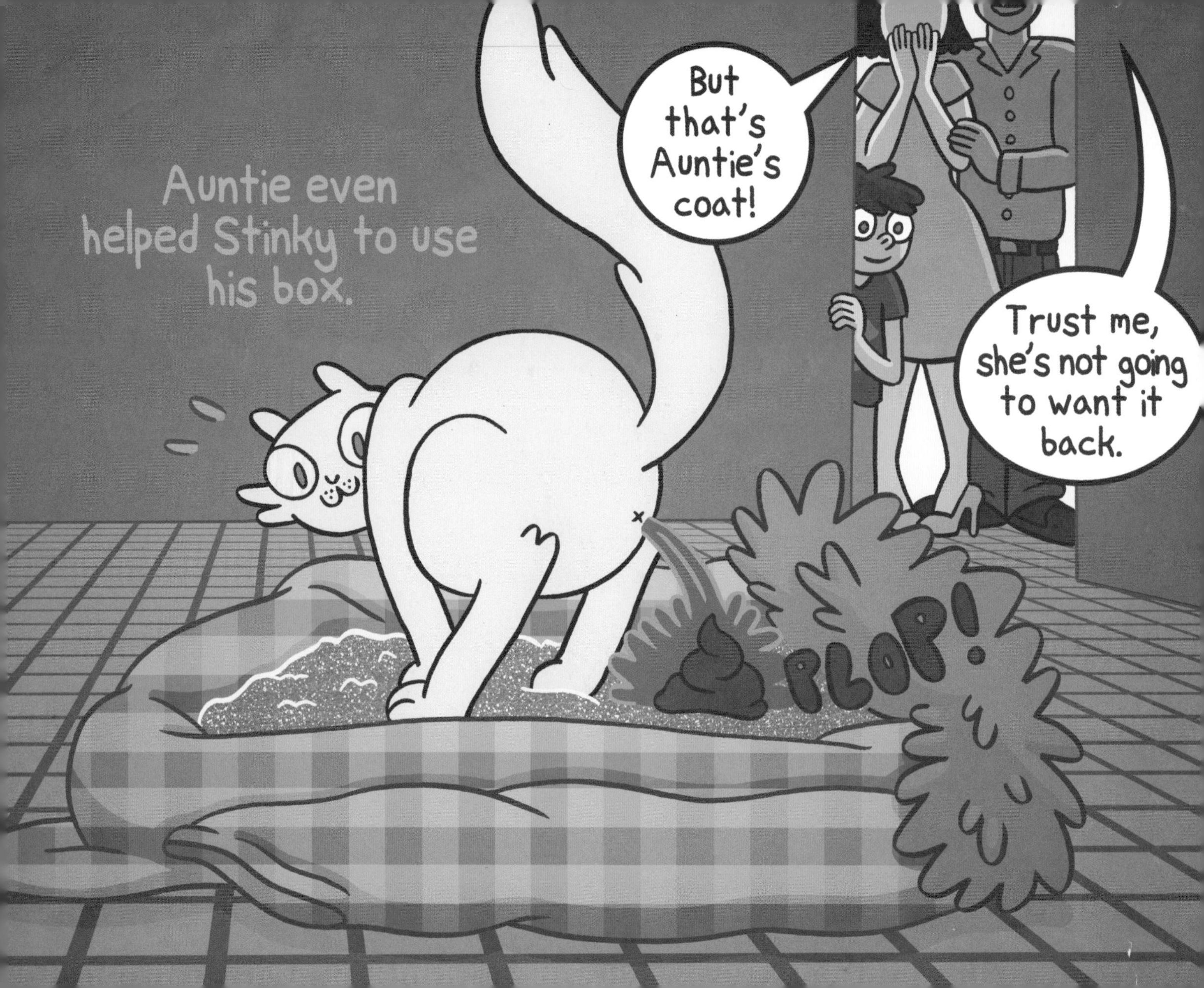
Auntie even helped Stinky to use his box.
But that's Auntie's coat!
Trust me, she's not going to want it back.
PLOP!

Sophie Goldstein's first, only, and most loved cat was named Sammy. Sammy enjoyed beating up the neighborhood cats, eating broccoli, and lying in the sun.

Sophie is currently studying comics at the Center for Cartoon Studies in White River Junction, VT.

Her webcomic can be found at dcisgoingtohell.com or you can follow her Twitter @redinkradio.

Gene Ambaum's favorite cat was named Sammy, too. He was the greatest cat ever, a blue point Siamese who survived being run over (twice), rode in a stroller, and loved both chocolate chip cookies and bacon.

Now Gene has two cats: Tokyo (sniffer) and Maple (sniffee). When he isn't scooping their box, trying to give Tokyo his anti-depressants, or disposing of Maple's numerous kills, he writes Unshelved, a comic about a library.

Follow him and his cats on Twitter @ambaum.

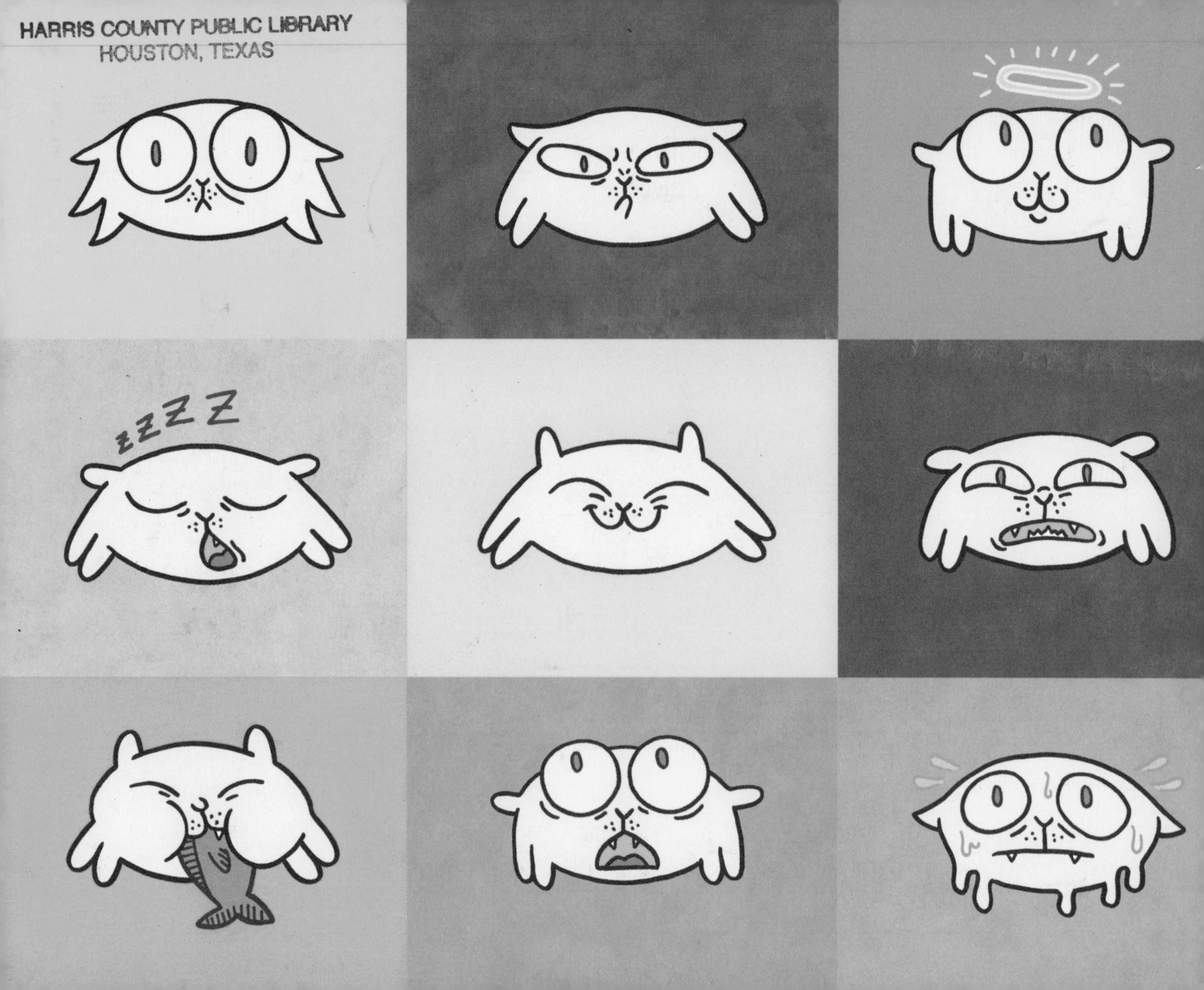
zzZZZ